WEST OF EDEN

Marshal Jack Adams was tired of people shooting at him. So when the kid came into town sporting a two-gun rig and out to make his reputation — at Adams' expense — it was time to turn in his star and buy that horse ranch he'd dreamed about in the Eden Valley. It looked peaceful, but the valley was on the verge of a range war — and there was only one man to stop it. So Adams pinned on a star again and started shooting back — with a vengeance!

MIKE STALL

◆

WEST OF EDEN

Complete and Unabridged

LINFORD
Leicester

First published in Great Britain in 2004 by
Robert Hale Limited
London

First Linford Edition
published 2006
by arrangement with
Robert Hale Limited
London

British Library CIP Data

Stall, Mike
    West of Eden.—Large print ed.—
Linford western library
1. Western stories
2. Large type books
I. Title
823.9'14 [F]

ISBN 1–84617–131–8

Published by
F. A. Thorpe (Publishing)
Anstey, Leicestershire

Set by Words & Graphics Ltd.
Anstey, Leicestershire
Printed and bound in Great Britain by
T. J. International Ltd., Padstow, Cornwall

This book is printed on acid-free paper

Prologue

Jack Adams stared at the toes of his boots, the heels of which were resting on the desk before him, and considered his future. A horse ranch, he thought, small but with blood stock. Maybe in Utah. Or better, California. That way he could visit San Francisco occasionally. He'd never been but he'd heard great things of it and he was tired of hick cowtowns and railheads. They even had an opera house there.

Lawson City had an opera house too, come to think of it, but it wasn't the same thing. Here, it was just a saloon with a (very small) stage in back. There they sang in Italian. That was culture. You didn't understand a word of it but you knew it was good for you. In the Lawson City Opera House you understood every word and the chorus girls could explain it to you later in the bedrooms on the second floor if you didn't. Not that much explaining went on.

Best of all, you didn't need to carry a gun in San Francisco. There were marshals and deputies but they were called the city police and they wore uniforms. If he ever wore a uniform here they'd put him on the stage too.

He was distracted by the heavy snoring coming from the back of the jail. First Deputy Bridger had arrested a drunk again last night. Adams was always discouraging that but it was a dollar an arrest and Bridger had a wife and two kids. And public drunkenness was against the law.

But so was half of what went on in Lawson City — at least, the pleasurable bits. He'd have a word with Bridger that evening. Not that it would do much good. He knows I won't boot him out, Adams thought, not over one drunk. Hell, he could do my job well enough. Will do it, probably, when I finally decide on that horse ranch.

Probably in Utah. Land was cheaper there and —

'Marshal!' Deputy Gilligan said, hurrying into the office from the street. The older man was almost out of breath. He'd obviously come somewhere near to running. Gilligan was the jailkeeper. Adams had been spelling him an hour so he could have a beer in the Lady Luck, Lawson City's other main saloon.

'Get your breath,' Adams said, not changing position. It was a hot, slow afternoon and not all Gilligan's haste could quite persuade him there was anything that urgent afoot.

Gilligan parked himself on the edge of the desk and tried to do just that. He sucked in breath, let it out noisily. Then:

'There's a kid in the Lady Luck — '

'A juvenile?'

Gilligan shook his head. 'Full growed, just about, and he's wearing a two-gun rig.'

'If six shots won't do it, it'll never get

3

done,' Adams pontificated, joshing the jailkeeper.

'He's talking bi — '

'Comes with being young.'

'About you. He's aiming to put a notch on one of them six-guns and on your account.'

'The left one or the right one?' Adams asked.

'Hell, Jack, be serious. I seen him draw. He was showing off — and he was fast. Very fast.'

'A dumb kid can draw his gun in a saloon all day for all I care so long as he doesn't shoot someone. I didn't hear any shooting.'

Gilligan shook his head. 'It ain't a joking matter, Jack. I got a feeling about this one. If he'd been just a kid and nothing else, I'd have taken his guns off him myself. I mightn't be too quick on my pins but I can still handle a Colt.'

Adams nodded. Gilligan was still a good man to have with you in a fight, especially with a shot-gun in his hands.

'But he'd seen my badge and he was

watching me out o' the corner of his eye. If'n I'd tried to draw I'd have drawn my last breath.'

'It's still talk,' Adams said. 'If I go and brace him, there could be a fight ... But he's in the right place. Big talkers drink big too. Let him be and he might just drink himself out. Then Bridger can put him in the cells tonight and make a extra dollar.'

'Be damned with Bridger and his dollar arrests!' Gilligan said, and then he shrugged. 'I've warned you, Jack. Maybe I'm wrong but he gave me a bad feeling.'

'Thanks anyway, Gilligan,' Adams said. There were plenty of that kind out there dreaming of making a rep' and a few of them even had longrider's rigs, but ninety-nine times out of a hundred it all boiled down to just talk — whiskey talk. 'Incidentally, I've more or less decided on Utah.'

Gilligan shook his head. It was an old game between them. 'You'd not last on a horse ranch, Jack. It's a dull, dull life. I — '

The shot rang out.

'It seems you were right all along, old-timer,' Adams admitted.

'I'll get my Greener and back you up.'

'No, there's only one of them so it only takes one of us.'

Gilligan didn't argue, knowing it would be useless. 'Watch him, Jack, this one's really on the make.'

Adams suddenly noticed that the toe of his right boot, at which he had been staring on and off for an hour but without really seeing it, was badly scuffed. He eased his feet off the desk and stood up.

'I'm always careful, Gilligan,' he said. 'That's the only reason I'm still here.'

★　★　★

'Marshal.'

The gunman called out as Adams left the jail. He was on the sidewalk in front of the Lady Luck which was opposite but just to the side of the jailhouse, well over thirty yards off. He was standing with both hands tensed inches away from his guns.

'Hey, what's the — ' Adams began.

But the gunman wasn't listening. He drew instantly, bringing his right-hand gun level with almost supernatural speed. Adams, who'd drawn as soon as he'd seen the hands move, only got his gun level after a bullet had smashed into the jailhouse wall. A second bullet, from the left-hand gun, tore into the dirt of the street six feet before him.

Adams didn't rush or panic. He knew that the speed of the draw or even having two guns didn't matter too much in a gunfight. What really did matter was hitting your target. And the gunman had made an extra mistake there. The range was too great. Most men missed with six-guns at ten yards or even less.

But Marshal Jack Adams wasn't most men. His first and only bullet caught the gunman in the sternum. Hitting bone and smashing it, the force of the heavy bullet was like a sledgehammer blow and the gunman was knocked instantly off his feet, the guns flying from his now useless hands. It was all over just a couple of seconds after it had begun. Adams reholstered his six-gun and walked slowly across the street.

★ ★ ★

He was dead, there was no doubt of that. The bullet along with fragments of bone had ripped through the nerve ganglia of the solar plexus. Adams always aimed for the centre of the torso. There were so many vital organs there that if you missed one you hit another. This time, as luck had it, he'd got him plumb centre.

Except in death he looked exactly what he was. All the bluster Gilligan had seen and heard had left him. He was just a kid. He'd scarcely begun shaving or needed to. His hair, no longer hidden by a man's hat, had the sheen and colour that nothing but youth could give it, and his eyes, glassy in death, were as clean and blue as a baby's.

Adams stooped to pick up the gun on the boy's right. It was almost new and there were no notches on it. Nor ever would be, at least of his cutting. Adams tossed it back down then looked away down Main Street towards the west. He wasn't looking at anything in particular.

'That was one hell of a shot.' It was Gilligan's voice, about ten feet behind him. They would be coming out of the saloons now to look, to clap him on the back if he'd let them.

He turned about. Seeing his face the spectators who had emerged into the street didn't think of clapping him on the back. Or even speaking. He walked back to the jailhouse.

'Make the usual arrangements,' he said to Gilligan, as he passed him without looking at him.

Gilligan just nodded.

They thought he was angry, Adams

realized, but he knew he wasn't. Nor did he feel guilty. The boy had acted the man he so nearly was and got a man's reward. He'd intended Adams's own death and he'd been lightning fast, the fastest Adams had ever seen. But he hadn't been a born killer, just a born fool.

Back in the jailhouse he stood before the desk for a moment, then stripped off his gunbelt and, a moment later, took off the marshal's badge from his vest. It was time to go and find that horse ranch. Or something. He'd had enough of such fools . . . and killing them.

In back, last night's drunk was still snoring contentedly.

1

I

Utah didn't make it. The bits he could afford were too hot in summer and too dusty as well. And it stood to reason that if Utah was too expensive, California would be no better. So he found himself moving north-west. Maybe Idaho or Oregon. Bad winters but there were fewer people and land was cheaper. Maybe even eastwards to Montana if he couldn't find what he wanted. It was a big country after all.

It occurred to him that he was becoming something of a saddletramp, but so what? It was good weather still and he had a decent suit in his saddle-bags for the towns as well as $2,000 in gold double eagles into his moneybelt. It wasn't a lot for a career in law enforcement but he'd been passing honest and anyway it was more than most people had ever seen in raw money. Not that they saw it or even guessed the tall, shabby figure on the big roan had more than a few dollars to his name. It was safer that way.

Adams wasn't even wearing his six-gun; he was keeping it in his roll. He didn't care to risk gunfights and having no gun visible was, he reasoned, the surest way to do that. Even his saddle sheath was empty, though he didn't take his new found pacifism to ridiculous extremes. He had a .32 cap and ball pistol in a leather pocket in his jacket. It was a Mexican gun but made by a real craftsman and if need be he could even hunt with it. Not that he did: bacon was cheap and beans cheaper and the accommodation charges zero, if you didn't mind the stars for a night light.

Last night he'd found himself thinking of the kid. It had been a waste but that was all. He'd done the right thing. With that kind of speed the kid could have gone on to kill a passel of folks before someone finally brought him down. It was his bad luck he'd tried to make his rep' quickly by taking on the more or less famous Marshal Jack Adams, not realizing that his rep' had been hard earned and that he hadn't killed a dozen men — outlaws and gunmen, all of them more or less skilled in gunplay — without knowing how.

In the end Wilson Smith — that had been his name, not even Wilse Smith! — had been no more than a straw. But he'd broken the camel's back nonetheless. Adams had just had enough of the gut-wrenching fear that came with facing another man's gun, and the feeling of utter emptiness you felt looking into the eyes of a man you'd killed.

Some lawmen grew to enjoy it. He never had, so now Bridger got the marshal's salary and probably upped it by arresting drunks at a dollar a throw. He'd get by too: he hadn't a rep' anybody gave a damn about.

It was high country, studded with stands of trees, and he nooned by one such, boiling unground coffee beans and frying up some bacon and beans. Afterwards he rolled himself a cigarette and stared down into the big valley to the west. Cattle country for sure, broken but lushly grassed. Yet in some nook in the valley side there might be a place.

He could ride into the valley and see, anyway. He liked the look of the land hereabouts — pretty far out from anywhere but still well ordered and peaceful.

He rolled another butt. There was no rush. He'd probably find a small ranch house and get a meal, oats for his horse and a straw mattress in the barn for four bits. Which even a saddlebum like Jack Vega could afford.

Need he bother with that name after all? This was the back of beyond and the slight exploits of Marshal Jack Adams would be a closed book here. But it was better to be safe than sorry, and it wasn't as if it were a complete lie. It was his name — John Quincy Adams y de la Vega. His mother was Castilian Spanish and that was the Spanish way of writing one's name. He'd just dropped the 'de la' along with the 'Adams', the former for convenience, the latter for concealment. Not all that honest but it meant he didn't have to wear his six-gun, and perhaps use it.

He finished the cigarette and scrunched the remains out between his fingers. Yeah, he'd go west, into the valley. He had a good feeling about it. It was a lovely place, as green and lush as you got, a little Eden cut off from the sinful world by time and distance.

He smiled to himself. Hell, I'm getting poetic. Too long alone. He hoped he found a little ranch house before nightfall and with it the chance of human conversation. He'd even be willing to talk about cows and their problems. In fact, he'd have to. Cow ranchers talked of nothing else, except for prices at the rail-head.

He collected his scant gear, cleaned it, packed it and mounted up.

'It's all downhill now,' he told his horse, which looked at him as if it understood and welcomed the prospect. Not that it did. Only lonely men talked to their horses and only the very lonely really believed they were understood, and he wasn't there yet.

'Maybe some oats tonight, old girl,' he said, patting the horse's neck, then he started down the gentle slope into the rich, green valley.

★　★　★

He heard the shot at just the same time as he felt the blow to his lower chest. Like a sledgehammer striking from nowhere and lifting him from the saddle.

'So this is — '

And then darkness supervened. And silence. After that one discordant note, the valley was at peace again.

To his surprise, Adams awoke. He was in the half dark of a bedroom, light sliding in through drawn burlap curtains. He was lying in a bed. He felt no real pain, just a soreness that seemed to encompass his whole body. He tried to move: pain like a knife stabbed his side. And his legs didn't seem to work.

His chest went tight, from fear rather than pain. Be calm, he told himself. He tried to move again, only a little this time, and found he could. The pain in his side was much less and the restrictions on his legs weren't organic but imposed by a weight of bedclothes. He put his hand to his forehead and felt a damp clamminess. The bed itself was damp too. The weight of the bedclothes fitted in — he'd had a fever and they'd sweated it out of him, whoever they were.

He remembered the shot, nothing else. It was a safe bet it had caught him in the side. He put an exploratory hand under the bedclothes, found himself bound up tightly. The bandages were damp but with sweat, not leaking blood. And they were about his lower ribs.

He took a breath. It came easily enough. If he'd been hit in the lung . . . but he couldn't have been. Hell, he thought, I'm going to go nuts speculating if I just lie here. Very carefully indeed he began to peel the bedclothes back. Even in the poor light he could see there were no bloodstains. When his legs were free he eased them ever so gently over the edge of the bed. The pain came back, but bearable now.

Can I stand? he asked himself. There was only one way to find out. Slowly he planted his feet on the floor and levered himself up. He almost fainted from the pain, but not quite, and after about a minute he was standing free on the wooden floor. Now —

He took a pace. And then another. His side felt now as if red-hot knives were at work, but the important thing was that he could walk.

Eventually he got to the window, tore back one of the curtains. All he could see outside was grass but the light itself was a benison. He noticed that he was wearing a nightshirt not his own — he hadn't packed one — and suddenly he realized something was missing — the money belt!

The hell with that! He was alive and that was by no means a minor miracle. And on the mend.

Suddenly weariness washed over him like the incoming tide and he knew he had to get back to bed. He edged towards it, almost falling, but in the end managed the few steps. He leaned over the bed, tempted to get back into it by the simplest method of all — falling — but realized strapped ribs would suffer if he did so. Instead he leaned forward more, half knelt on the bed and lowered himself down.

He finally lay across it on his belly, knowing that if he tried to prise himself up and into a more comfortable position he would faint away with the pain. But he could hardly stay like this, athwart the bed and half-smothering in the piled up blankets.

Yet stay he did, the problem solved for him by sleep which knocked him out more quickly and efficiently than the blow of a club.

★ ★ ★

'How are you?'

Adams looked up, saw a man's face staring down at him. He had somehow turned over in his sleep without waking himself.

'Weary,' Adams said.

The man smiled. He was middle-aged, in work clothes, with a slightly melancholic look to him. 'I see you've been up. How did walking feel?'

'It hurt.'

'I shouldn't wonder. You took one heck of a bash in the ribs.'

'I was shot,' Adams said.

'Yep. That was four days ago now.

Incidentally, I'm Tom Smith and this is my ranch.'

'Thanks,' Adams said, offering his hand. 'I'm Jack . . . Vega. But my clothes — '

'In that closet over there. Along with your money belt. It was that which saved you. It took the bullet, rode up into your ribs. The shock knocked you out, I reckon. My kid found you with your foot still caught in the stirrup out in the north quarter. It's woody that way so you hadn't been dragged far.'

'He saw the shooting?'

The man shook his head. 'Nor heard it even.' He paused, smiled slightly. 'So how did we know? I'll show you.' He went over to the closet, brought out the money belt — obviously still full by the way he held it — and extracted a double eagle. At least, it had been once. Now it looked as if someone had tried to make a washer out of it and hadn't quite succeeded. 'It took the force of the impact,' Tom Smith said. 'I reckon a ball from a Springfield at extreme range. You were very lucky.'

People always said that, Adams thought, except if you'd been really lucky the bullet would have just missed you, or not even been fired in the first place. 'Who shot me?'

'I don't know,' Smith said, cautiously.

Adams didn't press. It obviously wasn't Smith himself. You don't shoot a man for nothing and then nurse him back to health. Besides, Smith was a cautious man and cautious men don't tell tales easily. But Adams was good at getting people to talk, though that was for later.

'Help me up, will you? I want to get dressed.'

'It's bit soon.'

'I'll just go nuts lying here.'

'OK.' Smith took the battered gold piece, slipped it back in the belt and put that back in the closet. 'You won't be wearing that for a while. Your belly's just one big bruise.' He started collecting the clothes together.

'Is there a wound?'

'No, not to speak of.'

'So the fever . . . ?'

'It wasn't exactly a wound fever. Even with the bullet stopped the force of it darned near killed you. The fever was your body's way of fighting back, I reckon. I've seen it before.'

'In the war?'

Smith nodded but in such a way as to close the subject off forever.

'Have I said how obliged I am to you and your boy?' Adams asked, after a moment.

'No need for that. In these parts we try to be good neighbours. We're God-fearing people.'

'With some exceptions,' Adams said, as Smith put the clothes on the bed.

'Maybe you did look like a buck,' Smith joked. 'We do get them occasionally, wandering down from the trees. They make a change from beef, beef, beef.' He caught hold of Adams by the shoulders and eased him gently off the bed by stages. Smith wasn't a big man but he was a strong one, and gentle too.

'I'll help you dress.'

'I'll manage, thanks.'

Smith didn't argue. 'When you're done come through into the big room.' He nodded at the door. 'I'll have some stew warmed up for you. I reckon you'll be pretty hungry once you start.'

Now it was mentioned Adams realized he was ravenous. 'I really am obliged, sir,' he said.

'I'm only sorry it happened in our valley,' Smith said, as he closed the door behind him.

III

The stew was from the night before and the better for it. Adams devoured a plate of it along with a wedge of unbuttered bread. Outside, the early morning light was brightening and his spirits with it. He was weak still but that was all. The bruises would fade, the ribs mend. He looked to Smith.

'Who shot me?'

Smith pursed his lips. 'As I said — '

'OK,' Adams said, 'you didn't see it and all that, but you know. At least, who's most likely to have done it.' He paused. 'I'm not after revenge if that's what's worrying you.'

'I saw you weren't toting a Colt but — ' Smith broke off.

Adams answered him directly. 'The .32 in my coat was for self-protection, though little good it did me. It's an old cap and ball five shot with the chamber under the hammer empty for safety's sake, making it a four shot. You seem to know about guns, Mr Smith: would you reckon that's enough to go on the offensive with?'

'No,' Smith acknowledged. 'You'd do better even with a derringer.'

'No range,' Adams said, suddenly professional and, realizing it, added, 'I'm not wanted and the money's earned. I'm on the look out for a horse ranch and the valley looked peaceful . . . '

'It ought to be,' Smith said sadly. 'It's

called Eden Valley.'

Adams laughed. Smith looked at him.

'It's just that that's what I was thinking before I got shot — the lush grass, a little Eden. But somebody else had the same idea.'

Smith shook his head. 'It's named for the man who first settled it, Billy Eden. He has the biggest ranch.' He stopped.

'And he'd like it to be ever bigger?' Adams asked.

'We've had trouble recently. The beef price in Chicago went down a while back. A lot of new suppliers in Montana and Wyoming flooded the market and Billy Eden decided he needed more land. So the trouble started.'

'Killings?'

'No, but he's brought in a new foreman, a man called Gall. A gunman. Quite a few of the smaller ranchers are talking about selling out.'

'Does this Gall tote a Springfield?'

'I thought you weren't out for revenge?'

Adams laughed softly. Even that

hurt. Then, 'No, I'm grateful to be alive. I'll move on, to the west. I'm not about to find a likely horse ranch in these parts. But doesn't it worry you, Mr Smith? You're staying.'

'I don't carry a gun, Mr Vega.'

'It doesn't seem to matter anymore.'

Smith just shook his head. 'No, I won't carry a gun again.' He paused. 'I'll get about my work now, Mr Vega. My son's been doing double duty. Unless you need — '

'I'm fine. I'll need a day or so to — '

'A week, at least. Those ribs were good and cracked. Your horse could do with the rest anyway. Meantime, make yourself at home. We don't often have guests here and we count it a privilege.'

'The privilege is mine,' Adams said. But Smith was already leaving, going off to run his ranch.

* * *

Adams took Smith at his word and looked around the house. It was about as far as he could hobble anyway. And even without delving into its private recesses he was still able to build up a picture of the family. Smith had come out west with his wife after the war — there was a wedding photograph showing a rather pretty, dark-haired woman, presumably now deceased. There were no photographs of children but the set up was for two people, Smith and son. There was a handful of books — a Bible, a dictionary, a book on cattle diseases and one on the law of real property. All were well used. And there were no handguns in evidence at all, only a hunting rifle and a shotgun.

Smith was exactly what he seemed, a thoughtful, hard-working, God-fearing rancher of mild habits — a good neighbour, and, if what he said of the conflict in the valley was true, at risk of being dispossessed or killed himself.

Almost certainly the pot shot taken at Adams himself had been really intended for one or other of the Smiths. Shooting passing strangers gained nobody anything. And as Smith obviously hadn't the money — this wasn't a rich man's house — to fight in the courts, probably too distant and too corrupt anyway, being gun poor and disinclined to fight in that way, he was lost. Adams had no illusions that right would triumph in the end. Whatever triumphed was called right and nobody argued.

But it wasn't any of his concern. He was grateful for what they had done but there it ended. Hell, for all he knew, Billy Eden might have both law and justice on his side, though given his methods he rather doubted it.

Adams contented himself with another plateful of stew while he glanced through the local paper, a copy of which he'd found by the fire-place, presumably already read and about to perform an even more practical purpose.

There was nothing about any range war in it. There never was. A local paper lived on advertising and the local merchants would be waiting to see who won before joining them. Instead it was all state and local business, fêtes and the fund to improve the local church. All that he really learnt from it was that the local town was called Riverton, which rather suggested it was on the local river.

He considered paying a visit to the stables but his exertions, slight though they'd been, had increased the ache in him. And Smith would have fed and watered his horse, he knew.

He got to his feet, reeled a moment, then set off back for the bedroom where he eased himself down on the bed and, still fully clothed, lapsed into sleep.

★ ★ ★

'Hi, how are you?'

Adams opened his eyes and saw the son of the house staring down at him. Except it was the boy he'd killed in Lawson City come back to life — the same pale-blue eyes, the same hair, the same features except no longer flaccid but fully alive.

'Just bruised,' he heard himself saying. 'Thanks to you.'

'My pleasure,' the boy said, with the same slight touch of formality that characterized his father's speech. 'Supper in half an hour. Will you join us?'

'That'll be my pleasure,' Adams forced out.

The boy smiled and left.

Adams quickly forced himself into a sitting position, ignoring the aches and pains of his battered body. His mind was racing.

He hadn't seen a ghost — ghosts don't invite you to supper. And suddenly he remembered the name — Wilson Smith.

Smith!

There were a lot of Smiths in the world. He hadn't made any connection but what if Tom Smith had had two sons and one had left? He could even guess why. A father who hated guns, who fought shy of fighting, and a kid who saw the need for it. Adams could even guess the reason for a too quickly acquired rep' — so Wilson Smith could come back and change things.

It was an odd coincidence that Wilson Smith had ridden south-east and he'd ridden north-west but not an impossible one. Wilson Smith had ridden towards the centre of things, out of the backwoods, and he'd ridden into them for opposite reasons. Coincidence just meant a falling together of things, if he recalled his high school Latin correctly, and fall together they had. The only question was what to do about it.

He could be wrong so he'd go carefully. Wilson Smith was dead whoever's brother and son he was and was going to stay that way. Even if they found out he was dead and how, it was the famous gunfighter and marshal, John Q. Adams who'd killed him. He was just Jack Vega, a well-heeled saddletramp.

He stood up. He'd had no choice.

Wilson Smith had sought him out, fired first, given him no alternative. There was no reason to feel guilty.

Except, for the first time, he did. And he found himself wishing fervently that he'd taken the trail east towards Montana.

He took a deep breath, not even noticing the pain it caused. Play it careful, he told himself. Make sure. And then — tell the truth or just ride on? Either way the kid was still dead.

He walked over to the window and the bowl of water on the table to the side of it. He'd better wash. He'd been invited to supper.

IV

His name was Bob and his brother had been called Willy — short for Wilson, an old family name. He'd left home a month before, just after he'd bought a two-gun rig. Tom Smith had said he wouldn't have handguns in the house.

Neither of the boys had known the reason for their father's aversion to them and hadn't even asked, knowing they wouldn't be told — and tempers had flared. At least, Wilson Smith's. He'd be damned if he'd ride out everyday at the mercy of Gall's gunmen.

Bob had seen both sides of the argument. If you didn't wear a gun nobody could say it was a fair fight. And while Willy was quick, it didn't mean somebody else wasn't quicker. He'd tried to mediate.

They weren't twins for all they looked it. Wilson was a year older and conscious of the fact. He didn't take counsel from his younger brother. And his father had exasperated him.

'And so he rode off south,' Bob concluded. 'He'll be back. You don't get rich working as hired help.'

Adams said nothing, rolled himself another cigarette. It had been easy for him to get the boy to talk. It was one of the tricks you learnt as a marshal, if you

34

lasted. Bob wouldn't even have noticed he'd been rambling on.

Adams looked down the gentle slope that led down into the valley proper; they'd walked out past the corral fence as the boy proudly showed off the ranch. Hell, he thought, I'm in this deep I might as well go all the way.

'Your father said I'd been shot by a Springfield. Does Gall carry a Spring-field?'

'A Winchester 45-60,' Bob said. After so many indirect questions the direct one took him by surprise. 'Slattery's the only one uses an old cap and ball Springfield, prefers it to a Winchester or a Henry.' He paused. 'Heck, Pa won't like me saying that.'

'It's OK, I'm not out for revenge. I told your father that and it's true. Life's too short. But it's as well to know these things, like who to avoid.'

'Slattery's someone to avoid all right,' Bob agreed. 'But Gall's even worse. Like one of them fellas who wish all the world had but one face so he could stomp it.'

Adams smiled. Those weren't Bob's words but some local wit's. All the same, he knew the type. 'What about Billy Eden?'

'He's old. He wouldn't be employing the likes of Gall and Slattery if'n he weren't. Fought the Indians; married one too, so to speak, but nobody ever called him a squawman. At least, not to his face.'

'No kids?'

'He'd three boys. Fever got 'em all, and his Indian wife too. After that he married a white woman regular fashion but she died in childbed.'

'And the kid?'

'A girl, Helen. A couple o' years older than me. She went back East to school. Doesn't have much to do with the likes of me.' He said this last a little regretfully from which Adams guessed Helen Eden wasn't exactly ugly.

'So how do you feel about Billy Eden?' Adams persisted.

'He's got pushy, but I guess he reckons he has first dibs on the valley. All the same, we've our rights too and we aren't giving 'em up.'

Adams liked the simple way he said it, without bluster. Maybe he could have liked his brother too, in different circumstances. On a sudden impulse, he said, 'Bob, will you let me give you — '

'Heck, mister, Pa said I wasn't to — '

'Not money. I wouldn't insult you. This.' And so saying he took out the .32 pistol from his jacket pocket.

Bob looked at it almost lovingly, his hand involuntarily reaching out for it . . . and then drawing back.

'I couldn't. Pa wouldn't like it.'

'He doesn't have to know. Nobody does. But it might save your life.'

'No,' Bob said, 'it'd be a lie all the same.'

Adams slipped the gun back into its leather pocket. Maybe it was for the best. It hadn't done him much good against a rifle.

'Thanks all the same, Mr Vega,' Bob said. 'I appreciate it.'

'You saved my life, Bob. I think you can call me Jack.'

The kid smiled. 'Jack it is then.'

Adams realized he hadn't lit his cigarette. It was too late now. The fine, dry tobacco had all dribbled away.

'Well, let's go see to the horses. That's what we came out for.'

'I sure appreciate the help, Jack,' Bob said.

'Any time,' Adams said.

2

I

Adams left the Smith ranch feeling, for the first time in his life, a coward. He had said nothing about killing Wilson Smith.

It wasn't out of fear, not even out of fear of losing their good esteem as he never expected to see either of them again. He was riding to Riverton and out of the valley on the western trail. It was simply that he couldn't see what good the truth would do.

The chances were that they'd never hear Wilson Smith was dead. It had hardly been big news back then and hadn't even got into the Lawson City newspaper. The merchants didn't like that kind of news; it was bad for a town's image. And if it didn't get printed, it wasn't news. So why not let

Tom Smith go on thinking his son was alive out there somewhere? He'd got used to the pain of that so what purpose was there in telling him he'd died like a dog in the streets of Lawson City and worse, he himself had nursed back to health his son's killer? It would only hurt him more.

It was, Adams thought, as he rode the Riverton trail at a leisurely pace on his rejuvenated roan, a very good argument. He could find nothing against it. And yet it still seemed the cowardly option. All the same, he wasn't going back. He'd stock up on supplies in Riverton and head further west. Where, hopefully, people wouldn't shoot at him for nothing.

Then he heard the hoofs pounding behind him. A rig was coming down the trail — fast. He turned, saw a pair of matched greys coming at him at racing speed and edged his horse aside. Eden Valley was a mad place, he thought, and then the rig passed him and he saw it wasn't pure bad driving — the girl on the high seat had lost the reins. He patted his horse on the neck.

'Come on, old girl, let's see if you're up to it,' he said and set out after the rig.

If the country had been open the matched greys and the light rig would have beaten him but the trail veered around small stands of trees and the loosed horses followed it. One of the stands was pretty lightly wooded and Adams risked it, ducking under the low boughs but making it, to find himself just twenty yards behind.

He touched spurs and felt the roan, already going at a good pace, lean forward as if anxious to join the mad rush of those two fine greys.

He caught up with the girl, passed her, reached down and caught the reins of the horse on the left.

He eased back gently — he didn't want to upset the rig — and slowly but surely the pace fell as the right-hand horse matched its partner. Eventually it had slowed enough for Adams to bring them both to a halt.

He dismounted, leaned over to take the other rein and then took the two paces to where the girl was hanging on to the sprung platform still, ashen-faced.

'You OK?'

She nodded as if not trusting herself to speak.

'Let me help you down.'

'The horses — '

'Have had their fun. They won't be galloping anywhere this day.'

'I'll stay here. If I get down, I won't dare climb back up.'

Adams laughed. 'What spooked 'em?'

'I don't know. I didn't see anything.'

'You can bet they saw something.' He glanced over them. 'A matched pair, blood stock. Maybe a bit high strung for a rig.'

'You know horses?'

'Passing well. I've ridden enough. I'd like to breed 'em one of these days.'

'I'm sorry,' she said. 'I haven't thanked you yet. It was fine riding.'

42

'I just followed your lead.' He smiled. 'Better, *their* lead.'

She blushed. Her initial pallor made the reaction all the more charming. She was, Adams noticed, a rather pretty girl, trim, auburn-haired, grey-eyed and with nice features. The mouth was a bit set but that was probably down to circumstances.

'No thanks needed, ma'am. Happy to help out.' He paused. 'My name's Jack Vega.'

'Helen Eden.'

He nodded. So this was the enemy — no, he corrected himself, Tom Smith's enemy, or rather the daughter of the same. He wasn't here to take sides. 'We'd better get 'em moving before they decide they're plumb tuckered out. Want me to drive?'

'No.' After a moment she thought better of that very plain negation. 'I'd better do it myself. I — '

'Maybe you're right. I'll ride along if I may, just in case.'

'I'd be obliged.'

* * *

She was gentle on the reins and the greys now responded with all the enthusiasm of a pair of old workhorses headed for the knacker's yard. Adams's roan still had a little life left in her and he had to hold her back a fraction.

'Are you staying in Riverton?' Helen asked.

'Just passing through, ma'am.'

'Call me Helen, everybody does.'

'My pleasure, Helen, if a brief one. I'm intending to go west.' He didn't add that that was down to her father's hired hands who seemed to have developed a taste for random man-slaughter. Why complicate matters? He really was just passing through.

'You're a cattleman, Jack?'

'I'm on the look out for a horse ranch. Eden Valley doesn't seem to fit the bill.'

She half-smiled. 'Not exactly. It's a bit too lush. Just what you need for fattening cattle for market. Horses can manage on less.'

'I'll bear it in mind.'

She laughed, a sound like the wind on a glass chime. 'I'm sorry, I'm lecturing you on horses just after — '

'An accident, Helen. As a future horse wrangler I absolve you of all blame.'

She smiled. Somehow her mouth didn't seem set anymore.

★   ★   ★

It wasn't long before Riverton hove into view, a touch of rather squalid brown in the sea of green, and the conversation changed into a repetition of thanks and courtesies, and then they were across the bridge and into its very heart. Adams doffed his hat and watched a moment as she headed for the general store, before turning his horse towards the nearest saloon. He wasn't a heavy drinker but as well as being without a pistol, Tom Smith's ranch house had also been very dry indeed.

II

The bar was empty but open for business. Adams guessed it always was. He ordered a whiskey and five cigars, pocketing four and lighting the remaining one. It wasn't bad but the whiskey was. It was strong though and that served. He was still a little sore and the wild ride to recapture the rig hadn't done him any favours.

He drew on the cigar, considering whether to order a second whiskey. He rarely drank in the daytime and never went over a single glass, but for once he was tempted, he wasn't sure why.

An old man in a dark suit and with pure white hair entered. He didn't have to order. The barkeep set up a whiskey for him unasked. He sipped at it, put the glass down scarcely diminished, then looked to Adams.

'Passing through, stranger?'

'You could say that.'

'I could say anything,' the oldster agreed. He glanced around for the barkeep and, seeing him at the other end of the bar, turned back to Adams. 'I could even ask what the famous Marshal Adams is doing in this little village in the hills.'

Adams looked at him coldly but said nothing.

'I was in the store when Helen came in full of your praises. As I run the local newspaper I came over to investigate. And instead of the unknown Jack Vega, I find you.'

'And this goes in your newspaper?' Adams asked.

'Not if you're passing through, sir. This valley is on a knife edge as it is. The news that a famous gunfighter is here could push it over the edge. I've no wish to do that.'

'But you are curious?'

'I'm a newspaperman, sir.' The oldster paused, then, 'Hell, I'm really a storekeeper. When my daughter married, her husband came into the business and he's a good lad. So I decided to do what I always hankered after, run a newspaper. And as we delivered goods anyway I had a ready outlet for it. I just needed the printing press and — '

'How did you know me?' Adams asked, somewhat less than interested in the oldster's business, which sounded more like a hobby anyway.

'I was passing through Lawson City a year back. You were one of the sights — ' He broke off. 'Hell, I'm not trying to be offensive.'

Adams smiled. 'I'm not offended, Mr . . . '

'Campbell, Hamish Campbell.'

'Well, Mr Campbell, I really am just passing through. I've retired too, in a way. I'm looking for a horse ranch.'

'And getting shot and rescuing young ladies on the way.'

'How did you know about the shooting?'

'It's not that big a valley, Mr Adams. There are few secrets. Everybody gets to know everything in a very short space of time.'

48

'Including this?'

Campbell shook his head. 'I owe you a favour, Mr Adams. I've known Helen for a long time and I'm very fond of her.' He paused. 'My little paper has power of a kind, Mr Adams. Not really for telling the news but validating it. If it's not printed, it's not happened. Not officially. I like to think that by careful use of that power I've kept the peace here. So doing you a favour is also doing a favour to myself . . . Mr Vega.' And with that he finished off his whiskey in one gulp and left.

Adams decided suddenly against having another whiskey. He'd go and buy his few supplies, get directions on the trail west, and leave. He might make the next town before dark, if not it would be pleasant to spend another night under the stars. They seemed very close here in the clear, mountain air.

It was then that the cowboy walked in, a big man with a swagger to him, and a big Dragoon Colt worn high on his belt.

' 'Morning, Mr Slattery,' the barkeep said.

So this was the man who'd tried to kill him, Adams thought. Slattery didn't give him so much as a look. Why should he? He hadn't seen him well enough to recognize or he wouldn't have fired at all.

Leave it be, Adams told himself. You're moving on. What does it matter to you? But it did. Slattery had been willing to swat him like a fly and it didn't matter that he'd mistaken him for someone else. Slattery wasn't worth searching out, but as he'd presented himself here and now, Adams knew he had to do something about it to keep his self-respect.

The barkeep had put a drink on the bar before Slattery. Adams edged up to it, spilled it. 'Sorry, friend,' he said a little heartily. It was not subtle but subtlety was hardly called for.

Slattery turned to him, mouthing obscenities. Then, 'You can buy me a bottle to replace it.'

'Hell, friend, I was just being polite. You bumped into me.'

Slattery's face blotched with anger. If there had been a space between them Slattery would have gone for his gun and settled the matter permanently, but there was no room to draw the Dragoon Colt so he lashed out instead.

Adams avoided the blow and retaliated immediately kicking Slattery on the shin of his right leg with the edge of his heel.

Slattery virtually exploded — the injury wasn't bad but the pain was momentarily unspeakable . . . and distracting. He lashed out even more wildly. Adams blocked the blow and brought his clenched fist down hammer fashion on the side of Slattery's neck. It was a stunning rather than a killing blow, intended as such.

He followed it up instantly, sinking a right to the belly, just under the ribs where'd he'd taken the bullet.

And then it was all over. Slattery was on the bar floor vomiting, no fight left in him. It wasn't even necessary to take the gun off him. For the next ten minutes he would have neither the desire nor the co-ordination to draw it, let alone fire it accurately.

Adams looked to the barkeep. 'You let drunks assault your customers in this establishment?'

The barkeep was too astonished to reply. The fight had lasted seconds and one of the most dangerous and feared men he knew was left retching on the floor.

'Hell,' Adams said, 'I don't bear a grudge.' He tossed a coin on the bar. 'Give him a drink on me when he feels up to it. He'll need it. He's puking his current load all over your floor.' With that he turned and left.

Oddly, Adams found he didn't feel very good about it — he'd given the big gunhand no chance at all. But if he had, he'd have had to kill him. Besides, he thought, he himself was still sore over a week or so after the shooting. Slattery would only be sore for a day or so.

He untied his horse but didn't mount up, just led her over towards the store and its hitching rail. In ten minutes he'd be out of town. It was unlikely Slattery would even be on his feet by then.

III

It was a big store with a stove, unlit, in its centre, a table and a chair to one side, and shelves all around, loaded with dry goods. The counter in back was small and a youngish man in a brown apron was leaning on it while two young women — one of them Helen — were standing by the table talking.

Adams touched his hat to them and went over to the counter.

'How can I help you, sir?'

'A stone of oats, a bag of jerky and some bread. Oh, and two cans of peaches if you have them.'

'That we do. I've a new consignment

of corned beef too.'

'I'll have just the one,' Adams said.

'Right, sir.' The man looked to the other girl, presumably his wife, as if considering asking her to help, decided against, and turned back to the shelves.

Adams leaned against the counter and watched the clerk — Campbell's son-in-law going about his duties. He could afford a store like this himself, he thought, but clerking in it wasn't a job he'd take to. That said, it was a pretty safe profession and secure too. People always need store-bought things. If —

'That's him, Marshal. Over there.'

Adams turned, saw the barkeep entering the store. He wasn't alone. The three stopped just in front of the stove, a middle-sized but very intense-looking man to his right, and a middle-aged man in a blue denim shirt with suspenders over it and a marshal's badge pinned to one of them, on his left. The town marshal was wearing a one-gun rig and his hand was on the butt of his gun. The intense-looking man had a six-gun in his belt, no holster, and his hands were nowhere near it but Adams knew instinctively he was the dangerous one, very probably Gall himself.

Adams stood away from the counter so they could see he wasn't wearing a gun.

'You accusing me?' he asked.

'Looks like it,' the marshal said.

'Of what?'

'Of half killing my man Slattery,' the other man said.

'He was the drunk who attacked me in the saloon?' Adams asked. 'Heck, he's not hurt. He was the one wearing a gun, but I only hit him the once.' Adams felt no guilt at the lie. He knew from long experience that everyone lied in like circumstances. Besides, he could throw attempted murder into the scales should he choose.

'I reckon you'd better come with us,' the marshal said.

'Is this an arrest or are you a lynch mob?' Adams asked. 'I only see the one badge. Is that a regular posse you have with you?'

The marshal looked very uncomfortable, not so much in the matter of the law but because he sensed his life was on the line. Adams wasn't talking like a man who was afraid.

'This gentleman saved my life, Marshal,' Helen said suddenly stepping forward towards the stove. They'd scarcely noticed the two women's presence and the marshal didn't welcome it now, but Helen was obviously a woman of importance hereabouts.

'He only came in with me a quarter of an hour ago and I can assure you he wasn't drunk,' she continued, adding to the marshal's problems.

'Get out of the line of fire,' the intense-looking man said abruptly to her.

Helen turned on him. 'You don't give me orders, Gall. You work for *my* father and don't forget it!'

Then the other woman — Campbell's daughter — joined her. 'This is our store, Marshal. People come here at our invitation, unless they have a warrant. Have you a warrant, Marshal?'

The marshal shook his head. He was on the point of backing down but Gall steadied him.

'The mayor can issue one, can't you, Mr Mayor?' He was looking at the counter clerk, Campbell's son-in-law, who didn't seem any too pleased to be drawn in to all this. 'I reckon I could, if a responsible law officer issued a complaint.'

'Go ahead, Marshal,' Gall said.

The marshal hesitated. He wasn't a real marshal, Adams knew. In law he no doubt was but in fact he was a jailkeeper, OK for handling drunks and bawling out kids but that was all. And this was all very troublesome to him now, something Gall had pushed him into, and what he most wanted was a way out.

A door just behind the counter, half-hidden amongst the shelves, opened and Campbell appeared.

'Having problems, Marshal?' he asked.

The marshal just nodded.

'I was talking with our friend here in the bar just minutes since. Desmond over there can confirm that.'

The barkeep nodded, adding, 'But you left just before the fight.'

'True enough, Desmond,' Campbell said, 'but I stopped outside to roll a cigarette. I heard Slattery shouting, glanced inside to see him attacking our friend here. It was over in a second. Which is what you'd expect considering who he is. Don't tell me you haven't recognized your colleague, Marshal — Marshal Jack Adams, late of Lawson City?'

And the confrontation was over in that instant. The barkeep disappeared, the marshal made his apologies and left quickly, and while Gall glared a second or two longer there was nothing for it but for him to turn on his heel and leave too. The confrontation had turned into a farce and Adams knew why. Gall had brought in the law because in this one narrow particular he had known he was in the right. Slattery had done nothing wrong in the bar but to be there. So why not use the law? But he'd forgotten that the law in Riverton was a very weak instrument indeed, otherwise they wouldn't be taking pot shots at people only a few miles to the north.

He noticed Helen looking at him, oddly. And not kindly either. She turned to the storekeeper's wife and said, 'I'll be back and finish up later.'

'Surely.'

And then Helen left without a word to him. Campbell was talking to him but he didn't take it in. He hurried over to the door and looked up and down the street. Helen was walking further into the little township. He hurried after her.

'Helen.'

She stopped, turned.

'I wanted to thank you. For speaking up for me.'

Her face didn't soften.

'And apologize. About the name

business.' He considered telling her it really wasn't a lie, that he was John Adams de la Vega, but decided it wouldn't wash with her. 'I've given up marshalling,' he said. 'I thought a change of name would cut down on confrontations.'

'It doesn't matter,' she said coldly.

'It does,' he said. 'But I haven't had a very happy time in this valley. First the shooting — '

'You were the one shot at?' she asked, obviously surprised.

He nodded. 'No worse for it though.' That was a lie too, he was still sore and bruised, but in the long run it would be true enough.

'I'm sorry,' she said, paused, then, 'you can walk me to the hotel. You'll be wanting a room anyway.'

Adams didn't argue. Why not stay at least overnight? Gall was surely a bad loser. It might be safer to start out west at first light. 'Are you staying in town?'

'With the Campbells,' she confirmed.

'You could still have dinner with me,' he said.

She looked uncertain. Adams considered reminding her of the 'rescue' but rejected the idea as crass.

'I was very taken by the way you stood up for me in the store,' he said.

'I just spoke the truth.'

'But you didn't have to.' He paused. 'I've been dining with Tom Smith for over a week now . . . '

She laughed suddenly, briefly, the crystal laughter he remembered from the trail. 'Why not then? You can tell me all about being a marshal.'

'It's just a job. Your marshal here — '

'Johnson,' she supplied.

'Well, your Marshal Johnson could tell you all there is to know about being a law officer. It's thankless and dangerous and if you're lucky enough to grow old doing it you end up in some hick town with a star pinned to your suspenders, sleeping in your own cells to save money and on the make for every dollar you can get.'

She shook her head. 'It's nothing like that here,' she said.

He looked a question.

'He was never a marshal before. Everyone in this town has at least a couple of jobs. Marshalling is his second job.'

'And the first?'

'He's the town barber,' Helen said, laughing.

And Adams suddenly found himself laughing too.

IV

'Goodnight.'

The word hung in the air as Adams stood outside the just closed door at the back of the Campbell's store. It persisted because it really had been goodbye.

Well, there were plenty more fish in the sea, he thought with rather forced cynicism and turned towards the narrow alley that led back to Main Street.

They hadn't talked about marshalling

at all and hardly more about Eden Valley. Helen had gone back East to school and she'd talked about that and Philadelphia, but mostly they'd just chatted and quite often she'd laughed and he'd smiled . . .

But tomorrow he was leaving the valley and he wouldn't be coming back. By rights he should be on the trail now. Eden Valley was trouble and he'd had enough of that to last three lifetimes, and he only had the one . . .

The alley was dark and narrow and he had to watch his footing. Back in Lawson City he'd have been on the alert but he wasn't a lawman any longer and it felt good. It had been a good evening even if it was a closed one. Even if there weren't trouble Helen wasn't the wife for the owner of a small horse ranch. Things would be tight at first, and maybe for a long time. It wasn't an easy life nor a way to get rich quick. He'd need a wife, but she'd have to be country raised, inured to the life. But there was no rush for that. And, he reminded himself, there were plenty of fish in the sea.

He paused as he came out on to the lit street. He suddenly felt gloomy. Even the prospect of a soft hotel bed didn't please and the journey in the morning seemed a chore. He took out one of his remaining cigars and lit it with a lucifer, looking over the one-horse town as he did so — balloon houses made like sheds from two by fours, the bigger ones passing as stores and saloons by virtue of their large false frontages. Even the church down the street was just a white-painted barn with a rather ridiculous bell tower built on one end.

This was the edge of civilization imposed on the scarcely tamed wilderness, rough and false and yet he liked it all the same. He didn't need the stone buildings of Philadelphia nor the fancy boulevards of New Orleans. This was home.

He drew on his cigar. It had been a strange day — the wild ride to start with, the rather foolish fight in the saloon, the farcical confrontation in the store, and then this evening, totally different from the rest. He'd remember this day for a very long time.

He shook his head, tapped the ash from his cigar and started walking down Main Street towards the hotel, keeping to one side out of habit, in and out of pools of black shadow and then into the glare of oil lamps, thinking that in due time Riverton and the rest would have brick buildings and gas lighting and maybe even policemen in blue uniforms and helmets. Then the shot rang out.

He was just below one of the flaming oil lamps when it happened and he didn't just crouch down, he flung himself into the nearest pool of darkness.

More shots followed, three of them. He saw the gunflashes but he didn't fire back. They came from one of the alleys on the other side of the street, maybe forty yards off. As he'd felt the bullet of the first shot passing nearby he reckoned he was under a carbine at least. Certainly his .32 wasn't up to the job of returning fire effectively and he would only give his exact position away. Better to wait. And the fact that he wasn't returning fire or moving could be interpreted a success: they might think they'd got him. People tended to believe what they wanted to believe, most of all in a gunfight.

He heard a voice. 'He's down.'

'Come on, let's get out here.'

'No, I'm going to finish him.'

'Don't be a fool!'

The conversation was conducted in forced whispers which nevertheless carried across the now very silent street.

Nobody came. A few moments later Adams heard the jingle of harness and then the thud of hoofs and he knew it was over.

He breathed out in relief. That had been a close one. But a miss was as good as a mile.

It was then that the wailing started, a woman's voice screaming into the dark not in physical pain but something worse, a terrible, heart-rending grief. The bullets hadn't found their intended mark but they'd not been wasted entirely . . .

He found his cigar was still in his hand, the lighted part knocked off but the rest still smokable. He relit it with a lucifer and stood there, waiting, as the town wakened around him.

3

I

The town was in a hanging mood. One of the shots had penetrated the bedroom of Jimmy Castell, only son of the grain merchant. It was his mother who had found him. The heavy bullet had caught him in the neck as he slept and virtually decapitated him. Even the shopkeeper mayor — his name was Jason Keyes — had become animated.

It had been a good thing he hadn't been wearing a six-gun, Adams thought. Or returned fire with the .32. They had been, and still were, out for full, blood vengeance.

'You'll take the marshal's job,' Keyes said, looking straight at him. It was more in the way of an order than a request.

'No,' Adams said. 'I'm passing through as you know. But I'll take the appointment of special deputy — if that's OK with you, Marshal Johnson?'

They were all in the marshal's office, a one-room affair with a single cell — unoccupied — in back: the mayor, the marshal, Campbell, Castell and a couple of other merchants. And Helen, her eyes still red.

The marshal, the only one of them sitting, looked up. 'Fine by me,' he said gratefully. 'God knows, I can use the help.' He paused, as if reflecting on what he'd just said, and added, 'Considering your experience, you'll take the lead, of course.'

'I appreciate that, Marshal Johnson,' Adams said, 'but we can help each other. Your local knowledge will prove invaluable, I'm sure.' Privately he doubted it, but it kept him sweet and that might prove to be worth something.

'What are we waiting for?' Castell asked. He was a very ordinary-looking man but now his eyes were blazing with pure hatred.

'In the dark?' Campbell asked. 'We

can't do anything until dawn.'

'No posses then, either,' Adams said. 'This is just a township. The marshal can ask assistance from its citizens on its streets but he can lead no posses beyond its legal borders. And who would we arrest?'

'Gall and Slattery!' Castell said instantly.

'Prime suspects,' Adams agreed, 'but I can't identify either one. We couldn't try them here either.' He looked to Mayor Keyes.

'I can't try felonies,' the mayor admitted. 'I'm just a magistrate. 'We'd have to send 'em on to the county seat.'

'We needn't send them anywhere,' Castell said bitterly.

'No,' Adams said, 'no lynch law. We could all end up in jail. We could also set this valley alight. There's already trouble between the Eden ranch and the smaller ranches. Given what'll happen if we seem to take sides illegally — well, you all know how it could end: a range war.'

'The Eden ranch had nothing to do

with this!' Helen said suddenly, and rather tearfully.

'No one's accusing your father,' Campbell said. But no one else spoke up to validate the sentiment.

'We've got to do it legally,' Adams said, 'but believe me, we'll do it.' He looked to Castell. 'Get back to your wife, man. There's nothing you can do here for the moment and she needs you now.'

Castell bowed his head and, after a moment, turned and left. But he wouldn't stay quiet for very long, Adams knew.

'What do you intend to do?' Keyes asked.

'Tomorrow I'm going to the county seat with a letter from you asking the county sheriff to swear me in as a special deputy.'

There was a silence, neither approving nor disapproving. They were all angry and hurt but they could see he was serious. They'd go along with him, he knew.

'For now, everyone to their beds. It's where I'm going. It's going to be a long day tomorrow.'

One by one they filed out.

'Thanks, Marshal Adams,' Johnson said when they were alone. 'I need this job.'

'Consider it professional courtesy,' Adams said. 'G'night.'

★ ★ ★

Helen was waiting for him outside the jailhouse. 'My father had nothing to do with this,' she said.

'No one's said he had.'

'But Gall's his man.'

Adams let the words hang in the air.

'I thought you were leaving Riverton,' she said after a moment.

'I was.'

'But now you're staying for vengeance, because someone shot at you?'

'No, I don't care about that.' He paused. 'That kid was killed in my stead . . . You know I wanted to hang up my gun. One kid too many was dead already. Another's too much.' He paused, seeing in his mind the small body lying on its tiny bed, the once pristine white sheets dyed a darkening scarlet. 'I'll do a professional job but my reason for doing it won't be purely professional. Gall and Slattery or whoever, somebody's going to pay for that kid.'

Helen was silent a moment. 'I'm sorry about the boy too. I knew him. I know his family.'

Adams said nothing.

'Just leave my father out of this,' she said softly.

'If he's out of it, I won't try to put him in it.'

'Just leave him alone!' she said and hurried off into the dark.

Adams sighed. It had seemed easy. You just took off your gun and found something else to do. But it wasn't easy at all. Yet he'd do what he had to.

II

County Sheriff Saltonstall, an unsmiling fat man, had been unexpectedly reluctant to give him a deputy's badge. Adams, weary from the ride, had merely shrugged his shoulders and said that in that case he'd be forced to move on. Saltonstall could investigate the murder of the child himself, though the *Eden Valley Enquirer* and the county press might be interested in the fact that his offer to serve had been turned down, an interest that would grow if a lack of progress in the investigation sparked off a range war in Eden Valley.

'Hell,' the sheriff said, 'the Eden ranch is worth just thirty votes to me in the election. Last time I won by over two hundred. It ain't worth the hassle.' He paused. 'Quote me on that, by the way, and I'll call you a liar.'

'I've a poor memory for such things, Sheriff. Or you could call it professional courtesy.'

'Be damned to that,' the sheriff had replied, tossing him a special deputy badge. 'No pay, no facilities and you'd better be damn sure if you arrest anybody that you've the evidence to back it up.' He paused. 'But you're not big on making arrests, are you? Just on putting notches on your gun.'

'I've never yet spoilt a good gun that way, Sheriff. Don't you want to swear me in?'

'Consider yourself sworn.'

★　★　★

Helen had left town by the time he got back and, superficially, calm had returned. All the same, you could still taste the tension in the air. The smaller ranchers were coming into town more, talking more. Of Billy Eden there was no sign and his henchman, Gall, was likewise absent. It was even rumoured Eden was now having his supplies packed in from the county seat, cutting out the merchants of Riverton. Whether this was true — no one reported seeing pack horses — Adams didn't know, but it was a dangerous idea. It meant the merchants of Riverton had nothing to lose. If the murder of the boy wasn't solved it really could prove to be the fuse to a range war.

Marshal Johnson, leaning back in his chair, was proving to be a more useful colleague than Adams had anticipated. He did have the requisite local knowledge — in spades.

'In terms of men with guns, the nesters outnumber the Eden boys two to one, maybe more. But that's not the whole tale. Quite a lot of the nesters are just fathers and their kids and they're armed mostly with shotguns and the occasional cap and ball pistol. On the other side, Gall's been building a force of gunhands, not top drawer but effective enough. They'll fight hard for their boss.'

'Gall or Eden?' Adams asked.

'Eden pays the bills, but lately Gall's been running the roost. Talk is Billy Eden's past it, or drunk all the time. But I don't reckon any of that's true.'

Adams waited.

'He's a sly old coot and tough as nails. As it is, if there's trouble Gall's there to carry the can. Billy Eden can always wash his hands of him.'

'And the town merchants?'

'In their first flush of anger over the kid, they'd have fought. Now, I reckon they'll not see the profit in getting themselves shot.' He paused. 'Hell, neither can I.'

'Who can?' Adams observed. 'It's odd, it seems this valley's been on the verge of range war for a long time.'

'I can't deny that.'

'But nothing's ever brought it to a head,' Adams said. 'Why now?'

'You mean, why did Slattery take a crack at you?' Johnson shrugged.

'I don't know. In fact, from what I hear, he still denies it.'

'Don't they all?'

Johnson nodded. 'Before that it was just fist-fights. The guns stayed in their holsters. But who knows how anything starts?'

Adams shrugged.

'But if it really gets bad,' Johnson continued, 'I can tell you one thing for sure: don't expect any help from Saltonstall. He'll just sit there in the county seat and let it all burn itself out and then snuggle up to the winner. That's always his way.'

Adams had already gathered as much but he didn't say so. 'It strikes me if we can solve the kid's murder we can defuse the whole situation. Nobody likes a child killer.'

'Ten to one it was Slattery who actually fired the shot, but that's not evidence, just a bet. I don't see you're ever going to prove anything. In the middle of the night, nobody about, and all you saw was gunflashes.' He paused. 'Then again, you could just shoot him for resisting arrest.'

'How would that go down?'

'In town, probably OK; with Billy Eden and Gall, who knows? It could put the stopper in but then again it could also light the blue touch paper.'

'It's academic anyway. He's not likely to come into town and, sheriff's deputy or not, I'm paying no visits to the Eden ranch at the moment.'

'Oh, he won't be there. Gall'll have him in the eastern line shack. It's just a mile off the Smith spread. That's where he always exiles cowboys who get into trouble.'

'How many there?' Adams asked, suddenly interested.

'There'll just be the two of them. But you'd never get near. It's open country around there and Slattery is a dead shot with that Springfield rifle of his.' Johnson smiled mournfully. 'Usually.'

Adams smiled grimly, an idea forming in his mind. 'Maybe I won't need to get close,' he said. Then, 'I'll say this for you, Marshal Johnson, you know this valley like the back of your hand.'

'Hell, we both know I'm really only a marshal on Saturday nights, just to make a few extra bucks warehousing drunks. The rest of the week I'm the barber and a good one. Naturally people tell me things. Don't you confide in your barber?'

'I shave myself,' Adams said, leaving the jailhouse.

III

'No,' Campbell said, 'I'll not do it. I've never knowingly printed a lie in my *Enquirer* yet and I'll not start now.'

They were in the backroom of the general store, its walls also lined with shelves but ones sporting a mixture of paper, printing sundries and the overflow from the store proper, canned peaches, canned peas and various dry goods. The press itself was in the centre of the room, a remarkably small machine, almost a toy.

The paper itself was more or less in the same class, Adams thought, an eight-page affair with a circulation in the low hundreds at best. It almost certainly didn't break even, but it gave Campbell more than money: it gave him an occupation and a position of importance in the community. Despite himself, Adams could see why Campbell wouldn't risk that easily. But he persevered.

'It wouldn't be a lie. I'll make a statement to the paper. Then you're just reporting what a law officer is saying.'

But he could see that wasn't working. He added, 'Hell, it wouldn't have to be a full edition. If I could get just one copy in to Slattery's hands, that would do it.'

Campbell's expression softened a little. 'That might just be possible.' He paused. 'You're sure he's in the line shack?'

'Marshal Johnson is sure.'

'Then he is. Nothing much goes on around here without him knowing about it. And one copy isn't exactly an edition, is it?'

'No,' Adams lied. It obviously was, albeit a very limited one. Yet if Campbell liked to think otherwise, who was he to argue?

'When?'

'He'll have it by noon tomorrow. That suit you?'

'I'm obliged. But I'm not sure how you'll arrange it.'

Campbell told him. Adams just shook his head in wonderment — Bob Smith would deliver it. And he'd be quite safe doing so. The general store was also the mail office and deliveries were in its hands. It was in no one's interest to disrupt the mail so there was a kind of truce in that regard. The Eden ranch itself distributed copies to the northern nesters, while the eastern ones were the responsibility of Bob Smith. The pager wasn't exactly mail but here in Eden Valley nobody made the distinction.

'You're sure?' he asked. 'I like the boy.'

'So do I. He'll be safe.'

'Then go ahead. I'll make my arrangements on the basis that Slattery reads it tomorrow at noon.' He paused, then: 'He can read?'

'Oh, yes. He's a subscriber.'

Adams laughed. 'How much does it cost him?'

Campbell looked surprised. 'Nothing, naturally, it's a free sheet.'

Not that issue, not for him, Adams thought. But he didn't say it. Best not to let Campbell know that this time, there was blood mixed in with the ink.

4

I

Billy Eden wasn't annoyed with his daughter — he rarely was — but he did find her present attitude exasperating.

'You think I should just give in, hand everything I've worked for over to a bunch of nesters just to avoid the risk of bloodshed? Tell me, girl, how do you think I won this ranch — by asking the Indians, give me the land pretty please? There was bloodshed in those days, believe me. I've three great scars on my body to prove it!'

'I know, Father,' she said patiently, 'but Gall — '

'Is an unpleasant man, I know it. But he's *my* unpleasant man, just as this Adams fella is the nesters'.'

'He's not that.'

'Is he for us?'

84

'No.'

'Well then, he's — '

'You didn't see the Castell boy.'

'I've seen worse than that, Helen. When we fought the Indians I saw sights I'd rather forget. But we didn't give in then.' He paused, then, 'And nobody was aiming at the kid, and it wasn't done on my orders. As I hear tell, this Adams fella attacked Slattery in the bar for no good reason.'

'Slattery shot at him when he first came into the valley.'

'So he says. That wasn't on my orders either and Slattery denies it. I'm even inclined to believe him. Tell me, girl, if Slattery shot him, how come he was able to play Sir Lancelot and save you from your own runaway horses? As I recall, Slattery hits what he fires at and it stays that way.'

Helen had no answer for that. Billy Eden pressed home his advantage.

'Do you know this *lawman's* reputation?'

'A little,' she conceded.

'It makes Slattery sound like a schoolgirl. He's put more people in Boot Hill than the average undertaker.'

She flushed. 'He's not like that,' she said, ignoring not just the evidence but the possibility of such evidence.

Suddenly Billy Eden smiled. He was a middle-sized man, wiry and tanned, but his eyes were as pale as hers and no less bright with intelligence. 'Ah, you rather like him.' He rubbed his chin. 'You could do worse. He's certainly better than that Tolliver fella who came out from 'Frisco two years back with his ruffles and pomade.' He laughed, shortly.

Helen smiled despite herself, 'No, he's not like Horatio Tolliver at all.'

'All the same, I'm not giving up the ranch just because you like some fella. You wouldn't really want me to. Where do you think your silk dresses and your two-horse rig come from? The goodwill of the nesters? They'd strip you bare and steal your horses in two seconds flat, believe me. And the merchants in

Riverton are no better — worse, maybe. They'd do the same and smile at you as they did it.'

Helen didn't hazard a reply.

'You'd best keep out of town for a while, stay here. Or go visit your cousin at county seat.' He paused. 'Yes, that'd be best. If there's going to be gunplay, you're well out of it.'

'But — '

'It's for your own good, girl,' Billy Eden said, obviously meaning it. 'And don't worry about Adams. He can look after himself. But so can I.' he paused. 'I don't want a range war. I'm too old for it and it's too uncertain. Best just to let things settle down. And it's a weight off my mind if I know you're safe.'

'Yes, Father,' Helen said. The county seat was better than being cooped up in the ranch house and you got to hear everything that happened in the valley. Besides which, she was still a dutiful daughter.

II

Slattery devoured the paper as soon as it arrived. There was little else to do in the line shack. It had two main articles, neither of which told Slattery more than he already knew — the first reported that the famous lawman Marshal Jack Adams had been made a special deputy marshal of Riverton and a special deputy sheriff too, exclusively concerning himself with clearing up the Castell killing. The other item was an account of the 'murder' itself.

Campbell, the old fool, justified himself in calling it that, when it was obvious to anyone that it had been an accident, by some legal mumbo jumbo that it became a murder because it had happened in the commission of a felony — the attempted murder of Adams himself. Slattery didn't know much law but as it was set in print, he felt it was pretty sure to be the truth, and it meant they'd hang him if they could prove anything.

But as to who had fired that shot in the dark, that was another matter. As Gall said, if he kept his mouth shut and his head down, chances were it would all blow over.

Yet there was a tiny item in the 'Latest' column at the side. (Slattery didn't notice that was in perfect alignment and had been set up and printed at the same time as the rest.) It read:

WITNESS FOUND

Special Deputy Adams has announced to this journal that he has found a witness to the dastardly murder of the Castell child. He refused to name the witness saying the said witness was being kept 'under wraps' but that on the basis of his testimony he fully expects to effect an arrest in the very near future.

Slattery read the paragraph twice, then flung the paper aside.

'Hey, I haven't read that yet,' said

Boise Playette, the tall, dark Cajun who was his companion in the line shack.

Slattery ignored him. Playette picked up the crumpled paper, straightened it and glanced over it. He went straight to the 'stop press' item.

'Hey, I guess we might be having a visitor pretty soon, a lawman-type visitor.'

Slattery fingered the butt on his six-gun. Playette was hardly being tactful but he was speaking the truth. But famous or not, Slattery wasn't afraid of Marshal Adams. He hadn't stood a chance against him in the saloon but no one would have, not taken by surprise like that, and out here with a clear field of fire all around the line shack, he was certain no one could get to him. He'd even had a rifle on the Smith kid when he'd delivered the damned paper, just to be on the safe side. Gall had said no more shooting, but it still paid to be ready.

And, he suddenly realized, it paid better not to be in the wrong place at the wrong time. Sure, the line shack was invulnerable against just one man but a posse could surround it, turn it into a death trap. Then it would be stay inside and get shot or come out and get hanged. Gall would be very sorry and Eden might buy him a gravestone, but that would be the end of it.

'I'm leaving,' he told Playette.

'Gall won't like that.'

Slattery's hand closed over the butt of his six-gun. 'You planning to stop me?'

Playette shook his head. 'Gall said to watch your back, not to shoot you in it. Wouldn't have mattered if he had. If I ride with a man, I side with him.'

'Not with me,' Slattery said. 'I can go faster alone. Besides, you don't need to run. I do.'

Playette nodded. 'I'll ride back and tell Gall, but I'll take my time. Got any money?'

Slattery checked, then, 'Three bucks.'

'I got ten dollars,' Playette said, 'take

it all. I'll get paid at the end of the month.'

'Thanks, *compadre.*'

'One more thing,' Playette said.

'Yeah?' Slattery asked, suddenly suspicious again.

'Just don't tell me the route you intend to take out of the valley. I'm a poor liar.'

'I wasn't about to,' Slattery said. 'Are you staying on?'

'Till I get enough for a grubsteak at the month end. After that, no. And it's on account of you, too.'

'Me? Why?'

'Because you know Gall better'n I do and you're not risking staying. As I said, I ride with a man, I side with him. But I like him to side with me, too. Gall doesn't seem to be the type.'

'I appreciate that,' Slattery said, genuinely touched.

'So let's get your grub. Take as much as you can stuff in your saddle-bags.' He went to the store cupboard and took hold of the bacon. 'If you're going north you'll need all of this.'

'Just half,' Slattery said.

Playette cut it in half with the razor sharp knife hanging there for just that purpose. He added, 'Add flour for baking and — that old standby — beans!'

The saddle-bags were soon filled and then Slattery put out his hand. 'It's been good riding with you, *compadre*.'

'Me, too,' Playette reciprocated. 'I reckon I'll take a bit of shut-eye now. That way I won't notice you're not here. And as I can't see in the dark, I won't notice you're not here till tomorrow dawn.'

Slattery laughed. 'I'll be seeing you!'

Playette nodded, rolled a cigarette, ostentatiously not going out and so seeing which route Slattery took. It was hardly necessary: he already knew. When he'd finished his cigarette he'd ride back to the ranch and tell Gall everything and a little more — like how Slattery had pulled a gun on him and stolen his money. Gall would check that and find it true.

He picked up the paper. Gall would want that too. He wondered if Gall would go after Slattery. Probably not. As he was going east out of the valley, why trouble? And Gall would have other things on his mind, like finding a new number two.

As he'd said, he always sided with a man he rode with but he didn't ride with Slattery anymore. And it was a dog eat dog world.

III

Night was beginning to fall. The wooded slopes that led down into Eden Valley were turning into patchworks of shadow as the light turned auburn before edging into black. And then he saw him, labouring up-slope on a tired horse, intent on gaining the heights before settling down for the night.

It hadn't been hard to predict. The northern slopes were harder to climb and there followed a hundred miles of broken, hilly country, before you got to anywhere with a name used by anyone but cartographers. Slattery would go east, go the way he himself had come, Adams realized, and so he had, right into range of the marshal's office Henry rifle resting across Adams's knees.

Even in this light it would be easy to pluck him off the horse before he even knew he was under the gun, but Adams didn't want that. Maybe he did have a reputation for taking few prisoners but that was happenstance — they'd preferred to take a chance on their six-guns rather than in a court of law. He hadn't blamed them for it; it had been their choice; he'd just been better and luckier.

But now with Slattery he particularly wanted a prisoner. He reckoned Slattery had been under Gall's orders, that Gall had even been with him, but he knew the only way to convict Gall was through Slattery's mouth . . . and dead men tell no tales nor turn state's evidence. So he let him get closer.

He was very near now, sitting his horse wearily and still unsuspecting. He'd no chance to run. A kinder and a wiser man would have dismounted long since, leading his horse up-slope, at the same time making himself a poorer target and keeping the chance of a quick escape too. But nobody had ever said that Slattery was either wise or kind. He was a back-shooter and a baby killer.

Adams stood up, aimed the Henry rifle. 'Get off your horse, Slattery. Don't try and use it for cover or I'll blow your head off trying.'

Slattery swore but obeyed. The arrest would have gone smoothly if the much put upon horse, suddenly deprived of its rider, hadn't perversely chosen that precise moment to collapse. It was none of Slattery's immediate doing but it still gave him a chance to jump aside and draw.

He was very fast. Adams could have killed easily for all that but, wanting a prisoner, he was indecisive and Slattery got the first round off.

It was surprisingly accurate, probably more down to luck than judgement but it still sent the Henry rifle spinning from Adams's hands. Fortunately it caught the barrel so as to send the gun spinning to the left so Adams's finger wasn't caught in the trigger guard.

Adams reacted instantly. He drew. It was getting very dark now and he wasn't about to chase an armed man through country like this. Now he let his six-gun speak — he had been wearing it again since pinning on the first of his badges. He didn't try for any fancy shooting but just emptied the chambers at the dark shade on the hill slightly below him. It staggered and fell.

Adams sighed. It seemed he'd been dogged by bad luck ever since that Smith kid had called him out in Lawson City. Gall had gotten away with it.

Like hell! Maybe things had gone wrong here but the answer to that was to put them right. Sure, he'd lost a witness but so far only he knew it . . .

He reloaded his gun; he'd had enough practice so that the dying light didn't trouble him in the slightest. And then he walked down to where Slattery lay. He was very dead.

The horse too was in a bad way. Somehow it had broken a leg in the brief, violent collapse. Horses were fragile creatures in their way.

'Sorry boy,' he said, as he put it out of its misery. Only then did he reholster his six-gun.

5

I

There was nothing fancy about Eden House, its owner thought, as he looked fondly on it from the corral rail he was leaning on, smoking an imported Cuban cigar. His first house on this site had been built of sod but he'd had a balloon house built of two by fours erected when Helen was a child. Thereafter it had grown with additions and lean-tos. He could afford much better. The Lights of Lobo County had had a little brick palace built for them, with furniture imported from San Francisco, but he preferred to keep his money on the hoof, and for that he needed land. He'd been within an ace of taking over the whole valley just before the nesters started arriving in force. That was why he'd taken on Gall.

No killing, he'd told him, unless absolutely necessary. And it hadn't been. Just the sight of the toughs he'd hired on had enabled Billy Eden to buy up three of the nesters and the rest would have surely gone the same way — it was next to impossible to make a go of ranching with insufficient land and less capital. Then the whole valley would have done more than bear his name, it would have been his. The town would have fallen into his hands like a ripe plum . . .

But it had all gone wrong. The nesters had a champion now, this Adams, and that was enough. Of course, he could still fight. Adams was just one man. Saltonstall in the county seat would look the other way if it came to a range war, and just one gunman, however skilled and ruthless Adams was, wouldn't alter matters. But such things left a bad taste in the mouth and while he might take their land *de facto*, *de jure* was another matter — title to land wasn't really acquired just by a six-gun these days.

No, better to wait. The likes of Adams didn't stop in hick towns for long and then things would be back as before. He could nibble away at the nesters, get title, own the whole valley. It would just take time.

Gall wouldn't like it but he was just a hired hand. Of course, Gall didn't think so — he believed the promises about being given land. Fool! This was Eden Valley, not Gall Valley, and no part of it would belong to anyone but him.

He drew on his cigar. The question was, did he still need Gall? He would be easy to get rid of. There was paper out on him, a murder warrant from Wyoming. Gall didn't know he knew that as it was under a different name. But it was the same man and it would be easy to arrest and extradite him. Saltonstall was aching to do it, but he'd wait for his word, and the thousand dollars cash that would accompany it . . .

All the same it wasn't time to dump

him yet. Adams would move on and he'd still need a hard man to deal with the nesters and what better than one you could dump at no risk? Gall couldn't turn on his boss because who would believe an indicted murderer?

Yes, that was the way. Time and patience. It was a pity Slattery had had to spoil it by shooting at Adams — and missing! Of course he'd denied it, only fools admitted that kind of thing, and nobody ever admitted shooting and missing. So why had he done it? Not on Gall's orders: Eden believed that. The Smiths were last on the list and Gall had helped compile the list.

But there was no need to speculate. Slattery was a gunman and they were all stupid and vicious, like rattlers. That was all you needed to know about them — use them and lose them.

Exactly! Slattery was used up so why not have Gall kill him quietly? When the body was found, the nesters would get the blame and the heat would be off. Everybody would be happy but the merchants wouldn't forget that it was the nesters who'd started the killing proper. (The kid didn't count, being an accident.)

Yes, that was perfect. He wouldn't even need to pay Gall a fee for the job. Slattery had screwed up so, *ipso facto*, Gall had too. Though he might need some persuading.

Billy Eden crushed out the remains of his cigar and dropped it on to the dry earth. He was glad Helen wasn't around at the moment. Eden Valley was all for her in the long run, the very long run, but it was better she didn't know how it was being obtained. She was all for sweetness and light. Well, so was he, but it took more than sweetness and required very little light indeed to really get things done the way they had to be done.

Hell, he'd done much worse in the old days. He found himself remembering . . . and suddenly he was conscious of the lack of a gun on his right thigh. He'd stopped carrying years ago. He didn't need to. Now he thought it done. And he really didn't mind the change at all.

II

Nobody was getting shaved in Riverton unless they did it themselves. Johnson was closeted along with Adams in the jailhouse, to which no one else was ever admitted. Any business to be done with either was done outside in the street and then only after one or other of the pair had locked himself in the jail.

The universal view was that they had a prisoner they wished to keep under wraps — and even the cell window at the back was covered on the inside with a burlap curtain so inquisitive boys couldn't climb and look in to see who was there.

Gall didn't risk himself in the town proper but stayed on the other side of the river and sent in two of his men. He had a long wait. They were under orders to be quick but the saloons were tempting and they fell into that temptation, so it was late afternoon when they rode back and joined him, both somewhat worse for wear but still capable of speech. Gall had been fuming for the past two hours and had very nearly ventured into the town himself. If Adams was ensconced in the jail it was safe enough, he'd told himself, but locked doors unlock easily enough and it could have turned out that he'd be confronted by Marshal Adams.

He was wary but not exactly fearful of him. Marshals could build up big reps with back-shooting deputies and sawn-off Greeners. But he'd have no back up and killing a deputy was a mug's game, especially a deputy sheriff. They hanged you for that kind of thing. And Adams could get lucky. Better to wait. So waited he had, though at some cost to his patience.

'You drunken scuts, I — '

'Not drunk, boss,' Torson said, a

small man who wore a pistola rather than a pistol at his belt. He was an accomplished backshooter. 'Had to go into the saloons to get the gossip.'

'And?'

'Well, there's some dispute,' Williams said. He was a big man, fast with a six-gun, a miracle with a Henry rifle. 'The general view is they've got a prisoner. Some think it's Slattery and a fair few think it's you.'

Gall snorted. 'Any other candidates?'

'None serious,' Torson said. 'The truth is, they don't know. They don't even know who they're keeping the prisoner for. Circuit judge isn't due locally for weeks and no telegrams have been sent to the federal marshal's office. Maybe there's some arrangement with Saltonstall but nobody knows.'

'They've definitely got a prisoner?'

'Nobody's seen nothing,' Williams said, 'but nobody doubts it.'

'It's got to be Slattery,' Torson put in.

Gall didn't say anything for a moment, not because he disagreed but because he didn't. The damn fool had seen that fake paper and run just as intended — straight into Adams's hands. Running makes you look guilty and that was useful as they'd damn all evidence. But stuck in that cell with just the two of them, he'd talk. He'd do more: he'd say anything they wanted and embellish it to please them. And there was enough to talk about, especially if they promised him a sweet state's evidence deal.

'We've got to get him out of that cell,' Gall said.

'Sure thing, boss,' Torson said. 'Let's do it now.'

Williams nodded.

They were both game enough to try, Gall realized, but mostly because they were drunk, in which state they'd be more hindrance than help. Besides, three of them were far too few. Spread the blame. While a simple jailbreak was a crime, Saltonstall would fight shy of getting involved in a range war. Gall knew he needed every hand on the ranch in on it, and Billy Eden too. Spread the blame wide enough and it just disappeared.

'No,' he told the pair of them, 'we can't have all the fun. Let's get everybody in on the act.'

Both smiled complacently.

Damned sheep! he thought, as he smiled back.

III

Adams lay on the bunk in the single cell and smoked a cigar. The burlap curtain before the barred window filtered the light inelegantly but efficiently. It felt like twilight but that was hours off. It was remarkable how time slowed when you were waiting, sped up when you were enjoying yourself.

He laughed softly at the banality of his own observation. The profession of lawman just wasn't conducive to original thought. He'd done well to get out of it. Except here he now was wearing a badge again, playing the same kind of games.

The plan was to get Gall to commit himself. Or Eden. Or both. And to do it here, in Riverton, where they'd be at a disadvantage. He'd used the fake witness scheme once before. It had worked then, but it didn't seem to be working now.

Give it time, he thought. And indeed there was nothing else he could do or could have done. The town was a dubious ally, the nesters a dangerous one, and even together they were over-matched by Billy Eden, who probably had Saltonstall in his pocket. The trick was to let them make a mistake. Only it wasn't guaranteed to work.

He crushed out the butt of his cigar and considered having another. No, not now. He lay back on the bunk and let his mind wander back to the start of things . . . to a town much like Riverton but further back east, though it had been pretty much on the frontier in those days.

His father had been a lawyer, but he could scarcely remember him. He'd volunteered in the second year of the war — he had lived too far west for conscription — and he'd made the town and his family proud. He'd been promoted captain, won a medal, and died in the trenches before Richmond.

There'd been honour but no money. All he and his mother had was the family house. She'd turned it into a boarding-house and made ends meet that way. But the work had been too much for her. Adams guessed the heart had really gone out of her with her husband's death. The lung disease had followed on from that like night follows day.

The town hadn't turned their back on him. He'd been boarded out, kept on at school and, when he graduated — early — his father's old law partner had given him what was left of his patrimony: the leavings from the sale of the house after all debts had been settled — forty dollars. He'd even offered to take him on as a law clerk for board but no salary, but Jack Adams had had enough of scrimping. He'd bought himself an ex-Confederate cap and ball pistol for ten dollars, a twenty-dollar horse and set off west.

How easily he could have ended up like Slattery or Gall, a gun for hire. Or like Wilson Smith, killed in his first gunfight and forgotten. Maybe that was why he'd reacted as he had to that killing. Whatever, he'd been lucky. The marshal of a cowtown had given him a choice; move on that day or take a job, and he'd had a job to offer — sweeping out the jail — except a deputy's badge went with it.

Was it getting darker? Adams stared at the burlap curtain. Maybe. Just. He dug out another cigar, lit it. It didn't do any good, thinking back. All the same he could recall how proud his mother had been of his dead father, proud that he'd left to join a 'moral crusade'. Of course, he'd agreed with her, but still he'd silently wished Captain Adams had stayed Lawyer Adams. Crusades came and went; he'd have much preferred to have his father.

He suddenly found himself thinking about Helen. He hadn't seen her since that night. That felt like a loss and yet he hadn't met her before that day. It just felt as if he had.

She was in the county seat, he knew. Johnson knew all the gossip. Billy Eden had sent her there to be safe and on that point, Adams agreed totally with Billy Eden.

Hell, he was getting too attached to this place, and it was a mistake. Everything had been a mistake since he'd turned west into Eden Valley. If only he'd turned east —

No, that was wrong. It had happened already. Eden Valley had come to him in the person of Wilson Smith, not given him a choice, shot at him in the street in a vain attempt to steal something from him he no longer wanted — a rep'.

The more he thought about it, the

more it seemed to make a kind of sense. But he knew it didn't. It was all just chance, coincidence and —

There was a tap on the door. He stood up, his hand moving towards his gun.

'Adams, it's me, Johnson.'

It was almost dark, he noticed. Time for Marshal Johnson to take over. He shook his head, he wasn't sure why, and walked out of the unlocked cell towards the jailhouse door.

IV

The ground floor of what had been the original house was now just one room — Eden's parlour. He had a leather sofa there, a card table, a private bar and a large oil painting of a longhorn looking at the viewer with what obviously were intended as mad, rolling eyes but somewhere between conception and execution something had gone wrong and what came across was the impression of a boss-eyed milch cow. Nevertheless, Eden had paid fifty dollars for it and esteemed it highly.

He was on the sofa with a drink in one hand and a cigar in the other when Gall entered.

'Sit down, sit down,' he said. 'But pour yourself a drink before you do.'

'Later,' Gall said. 'We've got problems.'

'Tell me,' Billy Eden said.

* ★ *

'I agree,' Eden said, when Gall had finished his tale. 'It's probably Slattery. Not for certain but it's the safest assumption.'

'Not safe for me,' Gall replied.

'Why not? You didn't fire that shot at Adams when he first came into the valley. You weren't there.'

'Neither was Slattery according to him, but that story won't last. It'll turn out I ordered him to shoot. And in town too.'

'And you didn't?' Eden asked.

Gall shrugged. 'It doesn't matter. Slattery'll spread the blame all he can. Damn Saltonstall for caving in and giving Adams a deputy's star.'

'He didn't want to.'

'But he did, and he'll have to back him up.' Gall paused. 'Unless you threaten to expose him for being corrupt.'

'Me corrupting a state official? That's an unheard of crime. I'd never admit to that.' Billy Eden smiled at his own humour, but not without noting that Gall wasn't smiling. On the contrary, he looked worried. Too worried. Maybe it was time to dump him. Gunmen were two a penny after all.

'You can smile,' Gall said. 'You're safe, you think. When there were hard things to be done, you were never there: I was — '

'Calm yourself, Gall. It seems to me this Adams has got you spooked. Maybe there's no one in that jail after all.' Suddenly Eden laughed. 'In fact,

I'll bet there isn't — Adams has read you like a book and now he's playing you like an instrument!'

Gall went red in the face. 'I want what's mine and I want it now.'

'And that is?'

'The land you promised.'

Eden's smile died. Did this fool really think that he was going to give him any part of his land? But he only said, 'What use is land to you? It only ties you down here and from the way you're talking, that's the last thing you want.'

'We could all ride into town and take him out, show who's the boss in this valley. That's — '

'Kill a law officer?' Eden shook his head. 'That would be stupid. Think about it, man. Why isn't Adams out here with a warrant? Because he's no basis for one. Despite all the flim flam, he can't prove anything. But if we go in guns blazing that's evidence enough.' He paused. 'Besides, I don't reckon he'd be all that easy to kill.'

'We've got the numbers,' Gall said.

'Do we? You've a few tough *hombres* out there who'd do anything for money but most of them are still just working cowboys. You'd lose *them* on the way to town, in dribs and drabs. And if the merchants took Adams's side — and it was a merchant's kid who got killed — you'd find your somewhat depleted band under fire from a dozen rifles in second-floor windows.'

You not *we*, Gall noticed. It didn't matter. Billy Eden was right: the raid was too dangerous. Now he needed to get away, not fight it out.

'So buy me out!'

'Out of what?'

'My land, the land you promised me.'

Billy Eden scrunched out the remains of his cigar, lit another. Then, 'That was for a particular job. You were to get it when all the nesters were gone. They aren't.'

'That's not my fault.'

'I didn't say it was, but those were the terms agreed.'

'Change them.'

117

'Why should I?'

'Because I know everything — the deals, Saltonstall, everything.'

'Do you now? And do you think I know less about you — that little business in Wyoming, for instance?'

Gall went cold. He'd almost forgotten about it himself. His hand moved towards his gun butt.

'Don't be foolish. Saltonstall knows too. He was the fella who told me.'

'So you always intended to stiff me,' Gall said. It wasn't a question.

But Billy Eden took it as one. 'By no means,' he lied. 'It's always best to have something on one's partners. You'd have made a most acceptable neighbour.'

'But not now?'

'Adams is no fool. If Saltonstall found out, so will he. Then he won't need evidence to get a warrant.' He paused. 'I reckon it's best you leave, Gall. I'm sorry it's come to this, but it has, and there's nothing I can do about it.'

Gall suddenly realized that Billy Eden didn't give a damn whether he lived or died. It came as a shock. He'd never had any affection for the old man, he'd been no more than a means to an end, but it was somehow shocking to realize that lack of feeling was reciprocated. 'Where do you suggest I go?'

'North. Nobody'll follow you in the woods. Strike out for the Canadian border. Thereafter, the world's your oyster.'

'With no money?'

Billy Eden stood up, smiling again. 'The labourer is worthy of his hire. You've been a good top hand, Gall, and I'm duly grateful. I'll get you money.' He walked over to the picture, lifted it down from the wall to reveal a small wall safe. He searched his pockets, found the key and opened it up. Gall watched him fiddling about inside. Finally he turned, holding a leather money bag.

'I think you'll find this generous.'

'How much?'

'Five hundred in gold. That'll go a long way, Gall. Get you started up elsewhere — '

'You bastard!'

For once, Billy Eden looked shocked. 'You don't want it?'

'I want what I'm due!'

'I say what you're due,' Billy Eden said coldly.

And suddenly Gall snapped. It was all too much. An hour ago he had been a free man, without a past but with very much of a future. Now, this arrogant oldster felt free to treat him like a dog. He reacted in the way he knew best.

He drew and fired. The end of the barrel was almost touching the old man's chest and the force of the bullet hit him like a sledgehammer. In one instant he was a living man, the next a bag of old clothes spinning away, arms spread scarecrow fashion. The money bag flew up into the air and Gall caught it with his left hand before stepping over the smouldering corpse to get to the wall safe.

He was disappointed. There was no more money there, only useless papers. Eden had been giving him the whole of the ranch's float. It made the killing pointless, but it was done. And it would have been better if he'd used the butt, not the bullet. Everybody would have heard.

He stepped back over the corpse, making for the door. As he went, he wondered if he could blame it on Adams or some nester, but as he stepped outside and saw the faces of the three cowboys in the vicinity he knew it wouldn't work. Somehow, they *knew*.

No matter, it was a bad idea anyway. It was folly to stay here. Even if he could square this, Saltonstall knew about Wyoming and Gall knew he couldn't live with that. He needed to get out of the valley.

He didn't bother to saddle his favourite mount but walked straightway to one already saddled and tied off on the corral fence, waiting to be ridden.

None of the three cowhands made any move to speak to him, let alone stop him.

Very wise that. One more would make no difference now. And Billy Eden hadn't known everything. There were warrants out for him in Texas and Louisiana too.

So what? At least he had five hundred in gold and a gun in his holster. He could start over.

Damn the old fool to hell! he thought, as he turned the beast he had mounted and applied his rowelled spurs.

6

I

The charade ended when Sam Haig, one of the old Eden ranch hands, rode into town with news of the murder.

Some of the merchants were not best pleased when they learned the jail had been empty all along and while they didn't quite blame him and Johnson for Billy Eden's death, Adams guessed he wouldn't be the winning candidate in any election for marshal.

For himself he wasn't pleased but he was hardly troubled. Eden had picked his own foreman and if this was the fruit of that choice, so be it. Play with snakes: get bitten.

But none of that altered his duty as a deputy sheriff to investigate crime so, leaving Johnson to go back to his barbering, presuming he still had any customers, and taking a fresh Henry carbine from the office gun cupboard, he rode with Haig back to Eden ranch.

'Will I have any problems with the men?' Adams asked.

'No, Slattery and Gall were the real hard cases,' Haig said. 'The rest are just followers at worst. There'll be no trouble.'

Adams had guessed that already otherwise he wouldn't have risked it. But the main reason he was going wasn't for the law side, he suddenly realized, but because Helen would be there, sent for from the county seat. And then what? He had no answer so he tried another question.

'How do the hands feel about Gall now?'

Haig shook his head. 'The way they always did. Scared. He's a very dangerous man, Marshal. Be careful when you go after him. He's tricky and he's fast as a rattler with that draw of his. And he hits what he aims at.'

Adams said nothing. He had no

124

intention of going after Gall. As he reckoned it, he'd done enough already. A warrant for murder would catch up with Gall eventually. Billy Eden had been a somebody and the powers that be wouldn't tolerate his murder by the help. But he didn't say anything. Why justify himself to Haig, a man he could easily have been exchanging bullets with if things had turned out a little differently? No, he'd see Helen and move on. He still had a horse ranch to search out.

★　★　★

Helen wasn't there but most if not all the ranch hands were, standing around before the house yattering like a bunch of schoolgirls. They grew silent as he drew up, tied his horse to the corral rail and made for the house, Haig alone accompanying him.

The house itself didn't impress him from the outside. It was big but utterly characterless. Inside, it was like a cattlemen's clubhouse.

The body had been moved but a stain on the floor in front of the safe showed where the killing had taken place. The safe itself was locked.

'I've got the key,' Haig said. 'It was still in the lock.' He paused, then, 'I'll open it — '

'Give it to Miss Helen,' Adams said. 'Let's see the body.'

They climbed a flight of stairs, narrow and dark, came out on to an exceedingly narrow landing. Haig led the way into the first room off it on the left.

Billy Eden lay neatly arranged on an old box bed, still with his boots on. He'd been shot at close range — his jacket was half-burned off. He was already white and waxen. Adams noticed he wasn't wearing a gun. He mentioned this to Haig.

'He hasn't for years,' the old ranch hand said. He was more than a little moved.

'Yes,' Adams said. He couldn't think

of anything else to say. Eden was dead, Gall had shot him. There was no doubt. His job was now over.

And then he heard the sound of someone on the stairs — not the heavy boots of a man but the lighter footfalls of a woman. He walked quickly out on to the landing.

Helen stood at the top of the stairs, anxiety and fear wearing her face like a mask.

'He's dead,' Adams said. 'You don't want to see.'

'I must,' she said, and came forward.

Adams stepped aside. It was her house, her father.

She went and stood by the bed, gasping at the sight of the dead man, the wreck of the father she loved.

'Oh God,' she said, 'it's true.'

Adams went over to her. 'There's nothing you can do.'

And suddenly she was weeping and he was holding her. He held her like a child as she sobbed. It felt right. After a while the sobbing ceased and she eased away, looking up questioningly at him. Her eyes were screwed up and red still.

'It was Gall,' Adams said. 'It happened in front of the safe. It's likely enough it was robbery.'

'You won't let him get away with it?' she said.

'No,' Adams said, without even thinking about it, and realized his job wasn't over. And then she was weeping again, her face pressed against his chest.

II

Adams left to Helen's parting wave and sullen looks from the ranch hands still about. He had an Eden ranch Winchester .45–.60 in the saddle sheath in exchange for the office Henry and a very adequate supply of provisions in the saddle-bags. His enthusiasm was not excessive. It hadn't been Gall's shot which had decapitated the kid and he had seen too many murders to be easily swayed. Gall fully deserved the rope, no doubt of that, but let someone else drag him to it. But he'd agreed: out of weakness.

Except it wasn't exactly weakness to be influenced by a pretty face briefly turned ugly by tears. But if anyone but Helen had asked him . . . And even then he hardly knew her — and knew nothing would come of it. He mightn't even see her again.

No matter, he wasn't about to spend weeks or months on the chase. Both Helen and Haig thought Gall would go north, and there were good reasons for that. The hills and mountains and woods there were good cover and there were innumerable ways through them. A man could lose himself there easily.

Maybe an Indian tracker could trail a man there, but Adams doubted even that. Most trackers succeeded because they worked out where their prey was heading and then looked for sign, and didn't always find it even then. There was more hit and miss about tracking than was generally believed.

He had no idea where Gall was going, save far away, but he did know the only chance he had of catching him was if he went east. Even if the odds were against that it still made more sense to try there than where he had no chance at all, though he'd been careful not to mention anything of it to either Haig or Helen. It saved argument.

If he found nothing, why not retrace his steps for a while and then take a different turning out of Eden Valley? He hadn't decided but it was something to think about.

He should have got out of the marshalling game a long time ago. It was bad policy to stay in once you'd got a big rep': you became more of a target than a lawman. Better to raise horses.

★   ★   ★

He didn't ride hard. There was no point. Gall, if he had chosen this route, would be doing the hard riding and tiring his mount. He wasn't, Adams judged, the kind of man to give a damn about his horse and so unlikely to get the best out of it. It could well be half lame in a day or so.

Come to think of it, Gall had been foolish not to have taken a spare horse or set off with a miniature remuda of his own. But when you've just committed murder you don't think very rationally.

So why didn't I borrow a horse? he asked himself. And he knew it wasn't panic in his case, because he knew the reason full well: a horse had to be returned and the chances were he wasn't going back . . .

He tried to force the thought from his mind but somehow it just wouldn't go. He'd like to see Helen again but common sense told him not to think of it. She was a rich young woman now and he was to be distinguished from a common saddletramp only by his reputation as a gunfighter. Not to mention the trick of the imaginary prisoner which could be construed as contributing to her father's killing. Better to ride on, out of this valley forever.

Except every time he came near to making a final decision, he found himself holding back from making it truly final.

He knew why well enough. Helen. But maybe it would be better for her if he left. He'd be a living reminder of her father's murder if he stayed.

It wasn't quite a decision, but he reckoned it'd soon harden up into one. The more he thought about it, the more he could see it would be for the best.

III

The Smith ranch was half a mile off track but he found himself going there anyway. Smith had saved his life and was worth a goodbye. And the truth? If he were leaving the valley for good, he could well afford it — but could Smith? But he wasn't about his own business, he was still wearing a star. And there was always a chance Smith or the boy had seen Gall.

The small ranch house seemed becalmed in quiet as Adams rode up to it. Maybe no one was about. He was up to the corral fence and already dismounting when he saw the Smith boy, Bob, sitting by the far corner of it.

His hand went straight for his gun. No living man sat like that. He looked around and, seeing nothing, no one else, walked slowly over to Bob Smith.

He didn't need to feel for a pulse. The pallor of death was upon him. He reached out and touched the skin of his forehead. Two hours dead. Gall could still be here but probably wasn't.

Carefully, Adams edged his way to the house, pausing by the window, glancing in and seeing nothing. He stood by the door, listening. Again, nothing.

He went in low, quickly, gun raised. He saw Tom Smith lying on the floor in the shadow. His belly was a mess of drying blood. They'd both been dead for —

And then Tom Smith's eyes moved, and the lips worked, not producing any sound at first, then 'Bob?'

Adams went and knelt by him. He hesitated only a moment before saying, 'Dead.' He was tired of lies. He added, 'He didn't suffer.'

Tom Smith sighed. 'My fault.'

'Just wearing a gun wouldn't have made any difference,' Adams said. 'Not against the likes of Gall.'

'Not that. First shot. Not Slattery, me.'

Adams was silent, utterly taken aback.

'I saw you,' the dying man said. 'I knew you. I was in Lawson City a year back. You were pointed out to me. And then I got a letter saying what happened.' He gasped for breath. 'Not your fault, I know.' He gasped for breath again, forced himself on. 'I was out hunting a wildcat been troubling the herd. Saw you. God forgive, I took

134

vengeance.' The tortured eyes seemed to transfix Adams. 'Forgive me.'

'I do,' Adams said. 'I'm sorry about your boy — '

'My fault. Wild. Too strict. But I couldn't allow six-guns . . . '

What followed was drawn out as Tom Smith laboured for breath. It had been during the war. His best friend had been shot through both kidneys and in between screams had begged him to finish him off. In the end he had, with a cap and ball Colt — and taken against handguns forever.

'Forgive me, James, forgive me!' Tom Smith said.

'You did well, Tom,' Adams said, knowing the dying man was seeing his old friend. 'All's forgiven.'

Tom Smith said no more. A minute later he was dead.

* * *

It all made a horrible kind of sense now, Adams thought, standing over the dead man. That first shot hadn't been the start of a festering range war between the nesters and Billy Eden, but the understandable if misplaced vengeance of a father. God knows, he'd paid dearly for it. As for Slattery, Adams thought, I was the aggressor. But he felt less than guilty. Slattery had turned out to be a child-killing backshooter. All the same, if Wilson Smith hadn't come to Lawson City and effectively called him out, a whole series of tragedies in Eden Valley would never have occurred.

Adams took a deep breath. It would be very easy to let events overwhelm him with guilt, but it had all been waiting to happen. He doubted Billy Eden had really wanted a range war but by employing a man like Gall he had almost ensured it. Now it wouldn't happen.

As for Slattery, he'd tried to arrest him. And Gall had had no reason to kill both father and son. He'd done it for horses. Tom Smith had mentioned that in passing. He'd come to steal horses.

As Gall had had a very long headstart and the killings had begun just two hours before, he must have first gone north, changed his mind, decided to go east instead and doubled back, intending to take some horses here and run a string of them, changing from one to the other to make better time.

Yes, that was why he'd killed them both. To give himself time. With luck nobody would have noticed the Smiths were dead for several days. Running with a remuda he would have made great time, outdistanced any possible posse . . .

And it was the biggest mistake of his life. A remuda of horses left a big trail and Adams knew he'd follow it to the ends of the earth if need be.

Adams bent and lifted the dead weight up a little, dragging Tom Smith over to the bed, arranging him as decently as he could — the man who had first shot him, then nursed him back to health. He couldn't find it in his heart to blame him. Tom Smith had made just one mistake: he'd embraced pacifism, but not completely enough. In all truth, Adams liked him the better for that 'not enough'.

He went outside and picked up the boy, carried him inside to join his father. He couldn't afford the time to bury them but he could give their bodies the protection of the house. Ceremonies could wait; Gall couldn't.

As Adams finally closed the door behind him he shook the anger and horror from him. There was no time for it now. He had a job to do — and a man to kill.

7

I

Gall rode until the daylight was going and then made a cold camp in the hills east of the valley. He'd found good provender as well as horses at the Smith place and the fact that he'd killed two unarmed men in the taking of both only made his enjoyment the sweeter.

He carved meat off a cold roast and washed it down with whiskey he'd taken in passing from the northern line shack until his belly was full and his head hazy, then lay back on the ground and stared up at the stars. He enjoyed their cold distance — a thousand cold eyes staring down at Jonas Gall and not caring what he did. No more than he did himself.

He smiled slightly. It was a dog-eat-dog world and he was top dog. Maybe he'd only got five hundred in gold this time but there was plenty more out there for the taking, and easily enough too, as he'd proved this day. That old fool Eden had thought he could cheat Jonas Gall, and died for his pains.

As for the kid and his father, they'd always been too pious for his taste, ostentatiously not wearing guns. Well, now they knew what good that brought. Except they weren't around to know it! He laughed, softly, at his own joke.

Were the horses secure? He forced himself to glance around, saw they were, and lay back. He needed to be up early. Maybe that famous Marshal Adams would be leading the posse — but not eastwards. They'd be getting bogged down in the woods to the north as he almost had before he'd come up with a better idea. But probably there'd be no posse out yet: they mightn't even know the preachy old man and his whelp were dead yet.

It was a pity though that he'd never get to match himself against Adams. He owed that man pain. He'd been made to look small in the general store. Hell, it was a pity too he hadn't been able to ride into that lousy little town and take it apart. That would have been good. And that crummy little barber Johnson owed him a life too, but then his like were everywhere — worms, nothing more.

He'd better sleep. He needed to be up at first light and moving. He had less of a start than he might have. He needed to build it up, get clean away. Then he could pick the best of the horses and shoot the rest to stop them wandering back and giving him away.

He found himself thinking about Helen Eden. A good-looking filly that. He'd tried to court her when he'd first come into the valley. Oddly enough, Billy Eden hadn't forbidden him to as you might expect, almost encouraged him even. But to her he'd always been just hired help, and not the best sort as she'd made abundantly clear. Of course, Billy Eden had known that's how it would be: it had been his little joke: why forbid his advances when he knew his daughter would reject them out of hand?

Not that he'd really cared. She'd just been land — and money — on the hoof to him. He could get his fun with five-dollar drabs above the Grand Union saloon. They never held their noses in the air or nagged him as she'd have been sure to do.

All the same, it had been a slight on him and it was only half repaid. A pity she hadn't been around the house when he left. He could have taken his five dollars' worth with her for free.

But that was past. Eden Valley no longer mattered to him now. It was where he'd been and all that mattered now was where he was going. Billy Eden had been right. With five hundred in gold and a way of getting more strapped to his right thigh, the world was his oyster.

He lay back, looking up into the clear night sky, trying to outstare the stars.

II

Gall awoke late. It was well past dawn.

The whiskey!

He cursed vilely to himself but for all that there was no one about — just green hills all around, studded with copses. Why weren't the hills all covered at their tops? Some problem with drainage or maybe the soil. He smiled to himself — he was a good cattleman still, and one with an eye for the land.

His back ached when he stretched. That came from lying on the cold earth. In twenty years' time it might become a problem, not now. And it wouldn't be long before he'd find a nice soft bed, and a nice soft whore to warm it for him.

Hell, he could use a cup of coffee but he knew he didn't dare risk it. Smoke was visible a long way off. There was supposed to be a way of making a fire that was quite smokeless but he'd never yet seen one that was. Even the driest wood raised a plume of fine smoke.

Whiskey?

No, not now. He needed to make up that hour. He'd even eat as he rode, and he'd ride all day. He'd be utterly safe then. He went over, untied the remuda from the makeshift picket line and retied them for travel, then saddled up the roan and mounted up.

★ ★ ★

The meat left on the bone was dry and hard but still edible, just. He found himself recalling the expression on the kid's face as he killed him. Sheer frustration, quite comical. Young Bob Smith hadn't even tried to run, not that it would have done him any good. It must have been hard to live in Eden Valley without a gun. He smiled. It had been easy enough to die without one.

The father, on the other hand, had come at him with his bare hands. He hadn't thought the old bastard had it in him, but that had been pure hate and fury in his face, trapped gunless in his own house, his kid dead already and him knowing it.

Could I have handled it *mano a mano*? Gall wondered, and decided he was glad he hadn't needed to find out. Such fury was akin to madness and who wants to fight a madman? But a bullet in the belly had soon settled his hash.

He glanced up at the sun. A while off noon yet but maybe he ought to change horses, keep 'em fresh. He didn't: it was just too much trouble. He'd do it at noon, that would be soon enough. In the meantime he needed a drink. He reached for the canteen, thought better of it. He still had some whiskey.

Hell, it was near enough noon. There was nobody behind him anyway. Why not noon early, have a drink, rest up —

No! He'd wait till noon exactly. That way, if anyone were following, they'd noon then themselves and there was no risk of being caught up with. He laughed aloud at the thought. It was a triumph both of will and intelligence and he was proud of it.

He applied his spurs to the flanks of the roan. He might as well wear it out. That was the point of having a string of them tied up behind.

Hill succeeded hill, copse followed copse, sometimes clustering together so tight you could call them a wood. He skirted them all — he could get in one heck of a tangle with a string of horses if he went through wooded country.

Maybe he'd have done better just going north as he'd first intended? But that was even worse for trees, and boring country to ride through to boot.

He kept glancing up at the sky, avidly watching the sun rise towards its zenith.

III

Gall awoke with the hot afternoon sun on his face. He felt thickheaded. Too much whiskey. Without looking he let his hand reach for the remedy — the same bottle.

'It's empty,' Adams said.

Despite himself, Gall looked first to the pint bottle. Empty it was. Then he sat up and looked at Adams. He was standing twenty feet away, a Winchester in his hands but not aimed. Despite that, Gall didn't doubt that there'd be a round in the chamber.

His head cleared itself in an instant. Adams could kill him as he chose. But he was wearing a star. Maybe that would give him a chance.

He said, 'How the hell did you get ahead of me?'

'I knew where you were going,' Adams said. 'And a single rider can take short cuts a man with a string dragging out behind him can't.' He paused. 'I also knew there'd be a spare horse waiting for me, if it were needed.'

'So what now?' Gall asked. Keep him talking. He needed any edge he could get.

'Now you're going back to Riverton.

How is up to you.'

'You aren't going to shoot me?'

'I fully intended to,' Adams said. 'I saw the Eden ranch and the Smith place. But now it doesn't matter somehow.' He smiled coldly. 'Maybe you deserve the rope.'

'I'll not hang,' Gall snarled.

'Nobody believes it until it happens,' Adams said. 'Have you ever seen a hanging?'

Gall had, a lynching. It hadn't been quick. They hadn't even made it a proper slip knot so the man had kicked and kicked, soiled himself, gasped like some fish out of water and gone much the same colour. In the end they'd finished him with bullets. Better the bullet first. He started to get up.

'Keep your hands away from your gun,' Adams said, gesturing with the carbine.

'Sure thing. I'm fast but I'm not fast enough to beat a man with the gun already in his hands.'

'Who is?' Adams said coldly.

Gall finally got to his feet, letting himself appear a touch more unsteady from the whiskey than he really was.

'Go on then, get it done!'

Adams started to aim the Winchester.

'Hey, wait a bit. Aren't you going to give me a chance?'

'I was just taking you at your word,' Adams said. 'Now I suppose you want to draw.'

Gall shrugged. 'I'd give you that chance. Professional courtesy.'

'We're not in the same profession,' Adams said.

'I've five hundred dollars gold — '

'I could take that off your body,' Adams said reasonably.

'Don't you want to know who's the best?'

'I already do,' Adams said. He smiled suddenly. 'But you'll be better company on the way back if you're dead than if you're alive.' He tossed the Winchester to one side. 'Your move.'

Gall ignored Adams's hands, only watched his eyes. Cold, calm, expectant. The damn fool thinks he's going to beat me! I know I can beat him but I wouldn't have given him half a chance if I didn't have to. Gall suddenly felt supremely confident. His luck had held out again. It didn't stop him going for a bit of an edge.

'Hey, wait. The whiskey — I'm going to be sick!' Even as he spoke he was diving forwards and reaching for his gun at the same time. He felt his hand close about the butt, drew it, brought it up. He could see from Adams's eyes the speed of it had taken him by surprise.

One more sucker! Gall thought. Then he felt the first bullet hit him. It stopped his forward movement dead. He fired himself, saw Adams's hat fly off as if a sudden gust had just whipped it away, but Gall got off no more bullets. One after another hammer blows were hitting his body — two, three, four, five . . .

And then he was falling, backwards now, knocked erect and then back by the force of the heavy bullets. It couldn't be happening. Nobody was faster. Besides, such things happened to other people, not to Jonas Gall —

The last thing he saw was the sun, no brighter now than a candle in the dark. And then a puff of unseen, unfelt wind blew it out.

IV

Adams walked back and collected his hat. It had no holes in it. The bullet had to have come very close indeed though. Gall had been fast. Too fast. If it hadn't been for that stupid diving trick of his it could have turned out very differently.

Adams walked over to the body. There was no doubt Gall was dead. He'd emptied all six cylinders into him and not missed once. He'd been too good to give him another chance to fire.

In fact, it had been foolish to give him any chance at all. Some marshals would have let him have it with the Winchester, a slug in the head while he slept. He'd never approved of that nor done it either. But he'd never thrown down a Winchester before when he'd a bead on an armed felon so they could settle it with six-guns.

And because of that he'd never wear a star again. Not because he felt guilty about it — he didn't — but he knew he'd given Gall a chance he didn't deserve and that he hadn't done it out of any idea of fairness or even for vengeance, both of which were understandable if not justifiable reasons.

No, he'd done it because he'd suddenly realized how the trial and the hanging — there was no doubt of either conviction or sentence — would be for Helen. Keeping the horror of it all in her mind as Gall lingered a fortnight or maybe even a month in jail.

And no lawman should kill for such a reason.

* * *

He was only wearing the one badge, the special deputy's star Saltonstall had given him. He reached for it, unpinned it and slipped it into his vest pocket.

So it was finally over. A punk kid had tried to build a cheap rep' back in Lawson City only weeks before and death after death had followed, each more senseless than the last. Even Gall's. He'd died here and not on the gallows because one Marshal Jack Adams was no longer in control of his own emotions.

So what now? Bury him here, ride on, forget Eden Valley? It was tempting. But he couldn't. The horses had to be returned, the stolen gold too, and the borrowed Winchester . . . An accounting had to be made.

He turned away, walked over to the trees, sat with his back against one and lit a cigar, fumbling with the lucifer as he did so.

There was another and maybe better reason to have done with marshalling. That had been close, too damn close. At one time the likes of Gall wouldn't have got off even a single bullet . . .

He drew again on the cigar as if it

were life itself, memories of too many other such encounters flashing through his mind. None of them glorious but at least needful, that alone making up for the tightness in the belly, the taste of bile in the mouth, the stink of burnt gunpowder in the air.

And always a corpse leaking blood into the dirt, except however much you'd hated or feared the man before, and some he had hated with a passion, you always looked away from it as soon as you decently could.

No matter that your veins were tingling with the new-found joy of being alive, that the world was now painted over afresh in glowing, primary colours, you looked away. Maybe Gall wouldn't have cared, but he wasn't like Gall and never could be, thank God.

He drew once more on the cigar and then tossed it aside, took a breath and then forced himself to his feet. He had things to do.

The sooner he found that damned horse ranch, the better!

Epilogue

Helen Eden stood by the window in the dress shop and watched the entrance to the county sheriff's office intently. The saloon opposite would have been more convenient as a vantage point but no respectable woman would enter a saloon. She recalled her father, not a fancily educated man but a considerable reader on winter evenings, telling her that among the Ancient Romans a citizen, smelling wine on the breath of his wife or daughter, was empowered to whip out his dagger and use it to full effect. That seemed excessive even for a savage people but the penalties here weren't all that small either: women who frequented saloons had no reputation at all.

'Are you sure I can't help you with something, dear?' asked Florence Norris from behind the counter. 'There's a bolt of lovely floral print cotton just come in — '

'Just let me be, Miss Florence,' Helen said. 'I'm waiting for someone, not buying.'

'Ah,' Florence said, 'a young man.' And giggled.

Helen found herself annoyed, the more so because Florence was right, but she stopped herself from snapping back a cruel answer. The truth was it was Florence, not her, who was condemned to go on looking through the window at life, taking what vicarious enjoyment she could.

And then Jack Adams came out of the jailhouse, seeming if anything more purposeful than ever. She noticed instantly that he was not wearing a lawman's badge. He started down Main Street in the direction of the livery. Was he leaving already?

'Thank you, Miss Florence,' she said, and went to the door.

'Good luck, my dear,' the spinster lady said, smiling not a little wistfully.

Outside, Helen climbed quickly up on to her rig and started after Adams. He was just thirty yards from the livery when she pulled the rig to a stop beside him. He looked up at her, surprised.

'I — ' he began.

'Climb aboard,' she said, a little peremptorily. 'We need to talk.'

Adams hesitated, then did so. He didn't offer to take the reins and Helen drove, turning out on to the now deserted Riverton road but only for 300 yards. Then she turned to the right, on to a trail that seemed to lead nowhere. Finally she reached a flat piece of ground where there was room to turn the rig easily but she didn't, just stopped it. Neither of them had spoken in the meanwhile.

'You were going to leave without saying a word!' she said with some emotion.

'I'd already spent three days in Riverton. You could have — '

'I needed time alone, to mourn. You

had to know that.' She paused, but only briefly. 'I thought you'd wait. But you were going to run off. Why?'

Jack Adams looked at her. 'It was my fault in a way — '

'No,' she said fiercely. 'It was my father's fault if it was anybody's. He got old and afraid the nesters would swamp the valley. But they wouldn't have and they won't. None of their silly little ranches is really viable. You saw the Smith ranch, was it thriving?'

'No,' Adams admitted.

'You can't run a profitable ranch with two hundred head or less, it's impossible.' She shook her head. 'He didn't need Gall. He just thought that he did.'

'You know cattle,' Adams said.

'Of course. I may never have ridden to roundup but I've done everything else there is to do on a ranch and done it well. That includes doing the accounts. I also know who to bribe, who to ignore. But I can't run the ranch alone.'

There was a short silence, then, 'Are you offering me Gall's old job?'

She stared back at him angrily. All that stopped a furious torrent of words cascading over him was the fact that she noticed he was half smiling.

'I'm sorry,' he said after a moment, 'but would it work? It's hard to stay on after a killing . . . '

Helen said nothing but grasped the reins so hard her knuckles went white. It wasn't about the ranch. If need be, she'd sell up. She didn't want to but if that were what it took . . .

Yet it wasn't that. As for the killings, she was certain nobody would hold them against him personally. Not if he had a good reason to stay. And suddenly she couldn't hold the words in any longer.

'What am I supposed to do? Should I be silent because I'm in mourning for my father? Should I wait to be asked? But if I'd waited, would I have been asked?'

And she found she could say no

more. She could only sit there on the sprung driving seat of the rig beside him and feel the tears rolling down her cheeks.

Adams said nothing for a moment, not quite sure what to say. Then he told her about the Smiths. What had really happened to that family. If it had seemed terrible before let her see how much worse it really had been. Oddly enough, as he spoke he saw that the tears had stopped flowing.

'You're the only one who knows everything,' he said. 'It didn't seem to be anybody else's business.'

'It isn't,' she agreed. And then she added, 'But it was none of it your fault, John.'

And John Quincy Adams — not forgetting the 'y de la Vega' — found that he'd run out of arguments. And gladly.

'Heck,' he said, 'I really wanted a horse ranch.' He stopped, seeing her expression turn suddenly blank and realized again that women have no sense of humour about some things. 'But circumstances alter cases,' he added quickly. And suddenly she was in his arms and all the rest was forgotten.

He'd come home, to Eden Valley.